The Wickett Sisters

In Situ

The Wickett Sisters

In Situ

STEPHEN HOUSER

A Novel by Stephen Houser

Lionel A Blanchard, Publisher

First Printing

Hardcover ISBN: 978-1-7335858-5-9
Softcover ISBN 978-1-63944-886-9

Cover Art and Design by Vincent Chong

Printed in the United States of America

With respect and admiration,
this Wickett Sisters adventure is dedicated to
Sheridan Oakes, writer extraordinaire.

"Life is hilariously cruel."

—Bender the robot—
Futurama

CHAPTER ONE

The soil was pure clay. Pure Hell truth be told. Moshe Dayan was working on an archaeological dig he'd had active for several years. Located near the residential buildings of the Ben-Yehuda Kibbutz, the dig's modest size and its odd circumstances had spurred Dayan's interest and caused kibbutz leader David Ben-Gurion to spare the land from new planting.

Moshe had found clear evidence of an ancient Mormon settlement. He had discovered home foundations, farm implements, and even occasional written documents authored by active, faithful Mormons. At some point a village populated by these alternative Christian believers had thrived. Now it was gone. And had been gone for a very long time.

A hundred years? A hundred and fifty years? Who knew? Dayan had been unable to locate any record at all of who had inhabited the desert settlement. Demon gossip argued that Mormons had indeed settled there, claiming that only the brave pioneers who had survived in Utah could make a go of it in Hell. Lucifer himself had no knowledge of the secret town or who its inhabitants had been.

Moshe himself knew for absolute certain that the inhabitants had been Mormons. Early on he had found the Mormon Holy Grail, a set of golden plates identical to those that had been revealed to Joseph Smith by the Angel Moroni. Smith's plates had been taken back up to Heaven. The ones down here had been destroyed in a fire. But Dayan had lived to tell the tale, unlike poor Joseph Smith who had not.

So it was that Moshe, along with an on-again off-again assortment of volunteers from the kibbutz, spent his spare hours uncovering bit by bit the ruins of what he affectionately called South Salt Lake City. He and his folks worked carefully with brushes and trowels protecting and preserving the Mormon town, but it made for a long discovery process. Moshe had been at it for five years now. But who was counting? This was, after all, Hell. The original home of everlasting.

Not that it was an ugly or inconvenient place any longer. Driven by a fanatical dedication to improving everything down here, tens of thousands of Jews had joined the Ben-Yehuda Kibbutz. They had cleared hundreds of thousands of acres of land and had planted fruit trees, garden vegetables, wheat, barley, oats, and tobacco.

Hundreds of work crews had also been contracted by Satan to renovate New Babylon, the capital city of Hell. Streets and sidewalks had been repaired and repaved. Skyscrapers were cleaned for the first time ever. Old homes were modernized and new ones built. Water mains provided fresh and abundant water and efficient sewers served every part of the city. Food raised at the kibbutz was trucked to the city, plentiful and affordable to all.

The sky was blue, rain was abundant, and lakes the size of oceans had been created. For the first time ever, it was *fashionable* to wear skimpy bikinis. Not just because it was hot, but because tans had come into fashion. Coco Chanel was happier than she'd been in decades.

And Hell was crime free. Or at least it had been since the terrible murders of several streetwalkers by Jack the Ripper several years back. Things were quiet. Things were calm. Which was fine for Lucifer. And even fine with his wife Mili, Hell's greatest detective. She happily dedicated her time to raising her three children. Little Mardie, who was not little at all now, was nineteen. Sriracha, her oldest son, was ten. And Baby Jesus, her youngest, was five.

Little Mardie was not at home much. She was usually hanging out with her serious squeeze, Arie. He was a buff young kibbutznik who wanted to be a farmer. Sriracha was an incorrigible boy who tried to burn up everything he saw or touched. His efforts had accidently turned Moshe Dayan's Mormon tablets to ash, and while that had been forgiven, the constant lighting up of his cigarettes was not. He smoked three or four packs a day, being given as many as he wanted by Satan's office crew. They knew his mother disapproved, but Hell, this was Hell. Right?

Sriracha particularly enjoyed the brand that priests and rabbis reached for. Holy Smokes. Yes, it was corny, but Sriracha loved smoking them and always had a pack rolled up in his

T-shirt sleeve. Little Mardie got a smile out of that and thought more than once of introducing her brother to James Dean. She decided not to, however, since James was *the* archetype of young movie rebels and who knew how *that* would influence Sriracha, her own pint-size bad boy.

Jesus Morningstar was young and bright. He was pale and beautiful with long copper hair done in cornrows. He had freckles on his handsome little nose, which was an irresistible target for his Aunt Mardie's loud smooches. Jesus loved the wet popping sounds of those busses and had developed a decent imitation that he saved only for Mardie's nose. She laughed with delight when he kissed her nose and made the noises. They promptly took turns kissing each other's noses. It sounded a lot like they were bursting plastic bubble wrap. There were no admirers of their bizarre behavior.

There was a bit of sibling rivalry between Lucifer's sons. Sriracha loved to flick thin little flames at Jesus. And when no one was observing, he had once pulled his brother's pants off and incinerated them. Jesus, for his part, did not have any flame gift—as his father, sister, and brother did—but he had learned how to neutralize Sriracha's insistent flame game by levitating his older brother off the ground. He often left him floating so long that Sriracha's cigarettes filled his bedroom with smoke.

Jesus always let him down at that point. Except for one time when he had left Sriracha up in the air and hid under his own bed to take a nap. Mili found Sriracha floating and smoking, but she could not get him down and she couldn't locate Jesus. That night he forfeited his treat at his mother's Ben and Jerry's ice cream shop, usually a reward for the *good* behavior he demonstrated. For once Sriracha went and Jesus stayed home.

Mili spent most of her own time at the kibbutz. Lucifer was particularly happy visiting the kibbutz and on occasion he even helped with kibbutz chores. He'd recently found himself assigned to muck out some horse stalls alongside two former Israeli prime ministers, Shimon Peres and Menachem Begin. Over the couple of hours he'd done the unpleasant work, the Devil wasn't sure if there'd been more shit on the floor or flying through the air between Peres and Begin.

Moshe stepped out of the dig pit where he had been excavating all morning. He sat down beneath a young orange tree. All of the kibbutz's original citrus groves had been burned down years ago when the murderer of a young female resident had torched them trying to conceal her dead body. But hundreds of thousands of new orange, tangerine, lemon, lime, and grapefruit trees had been planted, and their vast greenery was a delight to Dayan's eye. His only eye.

His other one had been shot out while he was on a spying mission with the British during the Mandate. Much to his surprise, the dashing eyepatch he had affected afterwards magnified his love life into mythical proportions. God hadn't closed a window without opening a bedroom door.

Moshe took a drink of water from his canteen and thought about the fact that he didn't believe in God. Hadn't since the horror of the Holocaust. Of course, he was in Hell now, so it was somewhat hard to deny that there was a God. He'd settled on the satisfactory philosophical position of just not liking God, *and* being grateful that he was in Hell. Moshe grinned and poured some water on his face. A lot of things had gotten better down here, no doubt about it. But it was still damned hot.

A young man working on the dig walked up to Moshe. Short with dark skin and receding hair cut short, Udi was a handsome bachelor who worked in the library at nights and dug with Moshe during the days. He wore overalls without a shirt and heavy leather work boots.

Moshe watched Udi approach.

"Sorry to interrupt your break, Moshe," the young man said. "But in the corner of D grid Mrs. Morningstar has discovered fragments that warrant your inspection."

Moshe arched an eyebrow. Over his good eye. Sometimes he arched the eyebrow over his patch. Ben-Gurion hated that. Your eyehole is not inquisitive, David would complain. Stop that right now!

"What kind of fragments?" Moshe asked.

"It's hard to determine for sure since the bits are embedded in clay. But Mrs. Morningstar believes they are pieces of bone."

"Animal?" Moshe asked.

Udi shook his head.

"She's pretty sure that the remains are human."

Moshe stared at Udi. Then he stood up.

"Lead on," he said with an amused smile. "I've found unusual things here before."

Mili was kneeling, studying the soil in a far part of the excavation pit. She was wearing a white blouse, red shorts, and a pair of pink Nikes with low-top socks. Her body was slim, but curvy. The men on the dig secretly admired the turn of her calves and her muscular arms. Her blonde hair was pulled back into a ponytail. For a lady who looked to be in her mid-thirties there was no hint that she had successfully birthed three children in Hell.

Mili was examining bits of bone embedded in the orange clay. She poked at them with her finger, then picked up a dental pick that Moshe had given her and dug some out. She put them in her palm and stared at them for a long time. Mili had avidly followed Dayan's pet dig as he painstakingly uncovered the old and forgotten town that he confidently pronounced as a lost Mormon settlement. She was not persuaded. There were virtually no Latter-Day Saints in Hell as they tended to be decent and ethical folk. The only Mormons who landed down here with any regularity were moral stragglers. Venture bankers and politicians mostly.

Moshe walked up. He was only wearing shorts and sandals, looking tanned and fit. Mili said hi but didn't look up. If her sister Mardie had been present there'd be at least one Wickett sister staring at Moshe's six pack.

Mili stood up and pointed the curved tip of the pick at two small bones in her palm. They were linked at the joint and yellowed with age.

"These are human finger bones," she told Moshe. "Phalanges from the smallest finger." Mili curled her little finger up and down. "The pinky. The small tip is called the distal phalanx. Below it is the middle phalanx. And below that one is the proximal phalanx which connects the finger bones to the wrist."

Moshe studied the delicate bones that Mili was holding. He also studied her palm—yet another unorthodox interest of his—noticing that the so-called head line in her hand was deep enough to signal that her IQ was staggering. He shook his head in admiration and refocused on the bone fragments. He's seen a lot of bodies as an Israeli soldier, and a lot of skeletons as an amateur archaeologist, but he'd never been given a tutorial on finger bones before.

Mili handed them to him.

"Is this area possibly the graveyard for your mystery settlement?" she asked.

"Yes," Moshe answered. "And early evidence suggests that the cemetery is actually a mass interment."

Mili frowned.

"What will you do next?" she asked.

"We'll cut a narrow trench through the burials and see what the baulk looks like."

Mili looked puzzled.

Moshe explained.

"The baulk is the soil wall created when the trench is dug. In it we can see the contents of the grid. Destruction layers, burns, graves, soil changes, and so forth. This layer upon layer depositing process is called stratification. The baulk wall then is a map of time past. Revealing history, tragedy—and as you can see here—death and burial."

"So, the massive number of bones buried together here may be the record of a massacre," Mili said grimly.

"Indeed," Moshe replied. "The trial trench and its resulting baulk will give us clues as to what we may find when we excavate the rest of the bones."

"Like bullets?" Mili asked.

"Bullets, knives, arrowheads. Bones cut, dented, and severed. All clues as to what may have befallen the people buried here."

Mili nodded.

"When do you think you'll start the trial trench?"

"This afternoon."

"May I watch?"

"You may *help* if you like," Moshe encouraged her. "Carting off the rubble from the new trench. You can keep all the bones you find."

"All right," Mili said. "Will you join me and Lucifer for dinner after we're done?"

"With pleasure," Moshe answered and nodded pleasantly.

Mili checked her watch.

"Let me call Lucifer. I need to tell him that he's on babysitting patrol until suppertime."

"Can't Mardie spell him?" Moshe asked.

"I'll call her after I talk to Lucifer," Mili told him. "I'd actually like to have her come out to the kibbutz and join us."

"Ah," Moshe answered. "Because you want some help removing the bastardin' clay?"

Mili shook her head, her face serious.

"No. I want her to give us an opinion on the baulk and the bones. She has the kind of eye that might find the evidence to support your belief that the settlers here were massacred."

Moshe nodded.

"You have to admit that the mass burial itself is suspicious," he insisted.

"Yes," Mili agreed. "And the finger bones we looked at were *cut off of the hand they came from.* As though the person had lifted it to defend themself against the blow of a knife or a sword."

Moshe let out a low whistle.

"Time to dig the trench and study the baulk," he said.

Mili nodded. It would prove to be both a thrilling and a tragic task.

* * *

Cutting the trial trench was fairly quick work. Moshe brought over a small backhoe and dug a four-foot wide, eight-foot deep, and six-foot long trench. The clay was hard and tight and what was dug out of the trench was broken apart by Mili and Moshe seeking bones or artifacts. They were no longer in situ, but still valuable for what they could reveal about the history of the place. The rubble was carted off in a wheelbarrow by Udi and another young man from the kibbutz.

After the trench was cut and cleared Moshe climbed a ladder down into it. Mili followed him. The flat wall of the clay baulk revealed that the ground was indeed a boneyard. The bones were densely packed, revealing skulls with bullet holes in their foreheads or temples. Arm and leg bones that had been cut, smashed, or broken by clubs or axes.

Moshe looked at Mili.

"Your take?" he asked already knowing her answer.

"A massacre," Mili said in a voice that was barely audible. "A goddamn massacre."

A slaughter had apparently wiped out a people living in a settlement unknown in the history of Hell. Talk about a cold case. How could such a catastrophe have gone unnoticed? How could the guilty have gone unpunished?

Mili shook her head. Didn't matter. The murderers hadn't gone anywhere. They were in Hell and they'd be caught. *She'd* catch them, by God. Or without God. Whatever.

CHAPTER TWO

Lucifer and Mili sat at dinner in the kibbutz cafeteria with Moshe Dayan, David Ben-Gurion, and his wife Paula. Both Moshe and David wore short sleeve white shirts and black slacks. Mrs. Ben-Gurion wore a taupe-colored linen shift and brown sandals. Satan wore khaki slacks and a white Polo top. Mili had on jeans, a blue cotton blouse, and some white wooden clogs she'd bought from a demon who claimed he was Norwegian. *Fay dah.* The two-inch-high clogs were comfortable and allowed her to look her husband right in the eye. That was fun. For her anyway.

The evening's conversation had been dedicated exclusively to the archaeological evidence being produced on Moshe's dig. Bones and more bones. Ben-Gurion was appalled that the residents of the unknown town had apparently been wiped out.

"Any way to tell the age of the settlement?" he asked Dayan.

"There are ways to *estimate* it," Moshe answered, pausing from his dinner of free-range chicken, vegetables, salad, and homemade ranch dressing. "The bullets found so far are from Colt six-shooting revolvers popular in the American Wild West period. Roughly the 1870s through the early 1900s. There are also slugs from Winchester repeating rifles used in that same period.

"I think given the widespread persecution that Mormons faced in their early years, they would have felt it necessary to protect and isolate themselves *even down here*. Judging from the boneyard it is clear that they failed and were completely exterminated."

"And that occurred without your knowledge?" Ben-Gurion asked the Devil.

"I was completely unaware of these people and their town," Lucifer replied. "Though I don't really know how that could have been possible."

"With demons willing to be bribed," David Ben-Gurion responded, "*anything* is possible."

Mili nodded her head.

"Alas, that is true," she agreed. "The fifth column here is monetarily driven serving apparently endless customers."

"Like shopping for your clogs," Mrs. Ben-Gurion stated quietly.

Mili blushed.

"That's true," she admitted.

David jumped in.

"So then, it is likely that the demon population rendered services to the Mormons and were bribed to keep their arrival and their settlement private."

"Yes," Moshe commented. "But then who betrayed the Mormon presence and sold weapons to the folks who proceeded to slaughter them all?"

Mili nodded. Demons were the only gunrunners in Hell. And if they had sold weapons to the killers, then those black market profiteers would know exactly who had purchased the guns they had used to commit mass murder. Could those demons be identified? Could they be found? And if so, what would it take to persuade them to be helpful to Lucifer's wife?

Paula Ben-Gurion asked an interesting question.

"Why weren't the murdered settlers reconstituted with new Hellion bodies?" she asked Satan.

"Because those folks were massacred without my awareness," the Devil answered. "Buried and forgotten. Resting anonymously here on the south side of Heaven."

"Ha!" David Ben-Gurion exclaimed. "South side of Heaven! I like that. *And where are you, David?* my mother might ask," he said speaking in a falsetto voice. "*South side of Heaven, Ima,*" he responded and grinned mischievously. "Ay, she'd be fine with that," he said spreading his hands wide as if to settle the question once and for all. "Until she found out that the south side of Heaven is actually the north side of Hell!"

While the others were talking it occurred to Mili that most—if not all—of the members of the Illinois mob that had murdered Mormon founder Joseph Smith were also probably here in the south side of Heaven. Had they embarked on a payback against the Mormons in Hell?

Revenge was a powerful motive. And for that matter, who was to say that it wasn't the Mormons' very real fear of reprisal down here that had caused them to keep their little sanctuary secret in the lonely expanses of Hell?

Mili, Lucifer, Moshe, and Ben-Gurion went to Moshe's apartment for late coffee and biscuits. Mili always found Moshe's flat a little spooky, being decorated with his personal collection of mythical half-human beasts and monstrously-shaped antiquities smuggled down to Hell by demons who specialized in such assignments.

Pharaoh Tutankhamun had employed the very same boys in the 1920s to "rob" his tomb in the Valley of the Kings multiple times before Howard Carter was able to ensconce the remainder of the boy ruler's burial treasures in the Cairo Museum. Other satisfied customers who'd redeemed their precious personal treasures included Napoleon, several Renaissance popes, Andy Warhol, and Liberace.

After the demons had carted down Moshe's personal collection, their leader mentioned that it was only the second occasion that they had fetched these kinds of objects for a modern client. The first time had been a haul away of ancient artifacts amassed by Sigmund Freud. He had charged clients a significant fee to help him pay for his antiquities, thereby setting the precedent for gouging patients that psychiatrists had held dear ever since. Even the ones who didn't collect bits of the history perched on custom stands.

"Will you be launching a formal investigation into the massacre?" David Ben-Gurion asked Mili.

"Indeed, I will," Mili answered. "I told Moshe that I want my sister Mardie to partner with me as we have done in the past. There will plenty of trails to explore. Was Joseph Smith one of the town's inhabitants? Was his brother Hyrum there also, the co-founder of the Latter-Day Saints? And if so, were they indeed tracked down by their old enemies from Illinois? The very men who had murdered them once before?

"And who helped the Mormons?" Mili went on. "Which demons did they hire to bring supplies? Food? Water? Weapons? Did one of those devils betray them and supply arms to their enemies? Perhaps most important is whether these fallen angels knew about the massacre? Did they personally witness it? And if so, who were the murderers?"

Mili's voice was excited and her eyes gleamed. What for this group of kibbutzniks was a terrible discovery in the very shadow of their beloved home was for Mili the case of a lifetime. She fell silent and the conversation quickly turned to kids, the new citrus groves, and the Herculean efforts the kibbutz workers had made restoring the buildings and houses of New Babylon.

Inside Mili was boiling over with excitement. Her heart was racing and emblazoned in her mind was the picture of the two little finger bones she had held in the palm of her hand. Who did they belong to? Had they indeed been severed during the attack on the settlement? She chatted about her own children glibly and happily, but her heart was swept by dark emotional currents and her mind held visions of the bones of murdered Mormons entrapped in the clay crying out for justice.

* * *

The coffee and conversation continued until long after midnight. Mili excused herself early wanting to spend some time before bed researching the story of early Mormonism. She knew absolutely nothing about that religion save two random impressions. First, no one she had ever met had anything unpleasant to say about Mormons. Second, there seemed to be an anecdotal consensus among both Mormons and non-Mormons that the Latter-Day Saints founder Joseph Smith had been murdered in cold blood after fleeing from New York State to Illinois.

These two things were all she knew about Mormonism. It made her feel ignorant. Mili didn't like feeling ignorant. She set up the laptop she kept in her kibbutz flat and powered it up on the kitchen table. She made an effort to skip looking at email and focus on the search for Joseph Smith. Then Hyrum Smith. Then their time in Illinois. Where they both had perished at the hands of a mob. She was rapt by what she found.

Joseph Smith had harbored significant political aspirations. He and his brother had left New York State—driven out by hateful residents—and settled in the town of Nauvoo, Illinois. They were joined by thousands of Mormon followers. The town—suddenly filled with Latter-Day Saints—promptly elected Joseph mayor. He accepted the post, though he was already busy as the president of the Mormon church, *and* he was also running for president of the United States.

Mili learned the Joseph Smith had a significant temper. When the town paper, the *Nauvoo Expositor*, criticized him for his polygamy—he had accumulated eight wives—Mayor Smith ordered the paper shut down and a vigilante Mormon mob destroyed the paper's printing press. Rioting erupted in the town and Smith called out the town's private militia, some five thousand armed Mormon men he had recruited, to end the riots. They did. Then Joseph Smith declared martial law in Nauvoo.

The governor of Illinois received a flood of hysterical complaints from citizens of Nauvoo who were *not* Mormons. He ordered Smith and his brother Hyrum to stand trial in nearby Carthage for instigating the riot and for committing treason by illegally using private soldiers to enforce the declaration of martial law. They were both found guilty. Before they could be sentenced, an anti-Mormon mob attacked the jail where the brothers were being held, believing rumors that Joseph Smith's militia was coming to free him and his brother.

Somehow the Smith brothers managed to have pistols smuggled into their cell. When the first members of the mob began to break out the bars of the jail cell windows, Hyrum shot several of them. Then he himself went down. Joseph managed to shoot a half dozen more men while climbing out the window before he was shot and killed. So it was that both the president and the assistant president of the Church of Jesus Christ of the Latter-Day Saints had their leadership roles end on the same day. But not before extracting a dozen lives from their vigilante foes. Not bad for a couple of church officials.

Mili proceeded to explore links that provided contemporary newspaper accounts of the whole violent episode. Most of the reporters took the position that the highhanded Smith brothers had been the first ones to open fire. Well, Mili thought, that was hardly a fair condemnation. The townsfolks hadn't come to take Joseph and Hyrum out for tea and cakes. They'd come to murder them and neither Mormon was willing to go down without a fight.

Interestingly, Mormonism survived the death of its founder and went on to become an economic powerhouse in Utah. So much so that the growing Mormon militia took on regular army troops sent by the United States government to collect taxes on Mormon sales of whiskey and guns and fought them to a standstill for a decade.

This was a surprising and offensive move by the United States government considering that the Mormons' leader Brigham Young had just been appointed the first governor of the new Utah territory in 1850. The Mormons suspected that the real goal of the federal government's intervention was to suppress their practice of polygamy and they drew their guns.

It seemed to Mili that the early Mormons had to mount a constant defense of their beliefs and lifestyle choices. They repeatedly faced threats, violence, and murder. Whatever stormy birth Mormonism had experienced, every link Mili opened about the modern church showed that its adherents were law-abiding decent people.

In 2012 Mormon Mitt Romney had run for president and had been only narrowly defeated by the incumbent Barack Obama. For most Americans, Romney's religion had no impact on their decision to vote for or against him. Far removed from the times of the 1960 presidential election when many US citizens voted against John Kennedy simply because he was a Roman Catholic. If they'd known about JFK's many secret affairs, however, they might have changed their minds. He wasn't *that* Catholic.

To Mili's knowledge there were very few modern era Mormons in Hell. Their pious natures and good deeds had consistently earned them passage to Heaven. She'd have to check with her husband to see the official numbers of those who had been sent down here, but she thought the tally would be small. Compared to Southern Baptists anyway. They had enough folks around to stage Biblical reenactments at every available café. Why was *that?* she wondered. Who knew? It was probably all for the best, though. The Baptists could act, and if Mitt Romney were at all typical of Latter-Day Saints, the Mormons could not.

Mili looked at her watch. It was back three in the morning. Maybe kibbutzniks liked to get up early, but she was going to go to bed and refuse to stir until she woke up naturally. She texted Lucifer an update before silently slipping into bed next to him. He'd kissed her good night and had gone to bed hours ago.

Dearest!

Great to have dinner with you and all our favorite people. Ben-Gurion and his wife. Moshe Dayan!

Searching the internet has revealed that Joseph Smith and his brother, Hyrum,

were very politically astute and exercised ruthless displays of power often accompanied by violence. It is no wonder they may have wound up down here with some of their diehard followers, seeking to hide themselves from their many enemies.

The question on everyone's mind will be, of course, are they buried here? Equally pressing is which one of their enemies sought them out and murdered them?

Well, enough for tonight.

Love you now and forever.

Mili

She sent a copy of the message to her sister Mardie, and then texted her an extra thought or two.

Dear Mardell,

No, I am not snockered. I only get to use your full name when you are too far away to throw something at me.

Moshe's work at the Mormon dig has uncovered a mass burial whose victims were murdered by unknown assailants in an overwhelming sea of gunfire.

Have Pfotenhauer bring you out here tomorrow. This is the most significant crime that has ever been committed in Hell and no one knows a thing about it.

Don't show up before lunch. If you wake me before that I will call you Mardell to your face. Forever.

Love you,

Mili

Mili slipped into a lightweight cotton nightgown, got into bed, and pulled the covers up to her chin. She was completely worn out and glad that Lucifer was sleeping deeply. Rest—not more babies—was the agenda for the night.

CHAPTER THREE

Paul Pfotenhauer, Lucifer's personal driver and trusted chauffeur for his family, was standing next to his parked vehicle. It was a 2009 convertible Volvo C70 T5 with FWD, leather seats, fog lights, alloy wheels, keyless entry, CD (single disk), MP3, air conditioning, metallic blue finish with a black retractable waterproof convertible top. Satan had let Pfotenhauer pick out the new vehicle and Pfot had negotiated every detail. All that the Devil asked was that it be a Volvo.

Lucifer had agreed to the purchase of a convertible to take advantage of the sunny days Hell was experiencing, and Pfot always drove with the top down when he was on his own. As a result, his rather worn and wrinkled face had turned a very dark brown, making it appear that a big piece of beef jerky was driving the automobile around Hell.

He didn't care. Neither did his longtime girlfriend Nancy Davenport, a resident at the Ben-Yehuda Kibbutz. The thin and pretty-looking seventy-year-old liked Pfot's earthy looks and divine manners. She didn't think he looked like beef jerky at all. More like a nice grilled steak. Made her feel naughty *and* hungry when she cuddled up in his sunbaked arms.

Pfotenhauer was waiting for Miss Mardie to come out of her house. She had called him early in the morning and asked for a ride to the kibbutz at eleven. It was just a bit before that now on a cloudless sunny day. New Babylon looked beautiful and new. Sol should be proud to shine on such a magnificent city.

It reminded Pfot of the London building renaissance along the River Thames in the 1980s. The gorgeous avant-garde architecture and the beautiful clean river had not looked that pristine since Roman Londinium's Bluestone walls had reflected the shining majesty of the river. New Babylon's recent buildings were worthy of Foster or Geary and were filled with prosperous commercial enterprises. Not only had the appearance of Hell's capital city improved, so had its economy. The days of poverty and doom were gone. If you wanted a taste of what the old Hell was like you had to go somewhere on Earth. Like Brazzaville or Detroit.

Pfot watched Mardie leave her spotless little Victorian-style house and walk down the front steps. She looked young and stunning, having been restored to a gorgeous Hellion body after she had been shot to death by Jack the Ripper. She had shoulder-length blonde hair, shapely legs, and smooth, tanned skin.

She was wearing skimpy red-and-white polka dot shorts, white sandals, and an American retro halter top from the 1950s. It was a white affair with pleated cups, a strap across the lower back, and another one that connected the top corners and circled behind her neck. A very substantial amount of cleavage was showing, which actually made Pfot sneak a little grin thinking that Mardie may have been called to work on a murder at the kibbutz, but she was obviously planning to work on Moshe Dayan as well.

"Morning, Miss Mardie," Pfot greeted the lovely Wickett sister as she walked up to the car.

"Oh, my, Pfot," she replied. "The convertible today?"

"Yes, miss," he answered. "Such a lovely day."

"Indeed, dear boy. But, oh, so windy." She gently touched her well-combed and hair-sprayed hairdo.

"No problem," Pfot replied dutifully. "I will put the top up right after you pop in."

Mardie smiled and winked at her octogenarian driver. My, he had gotten brown. Looked like a Christmas gingerbread boy. Pfot held her door open while she climbed in the back. Then he shut it and got in the driver's seat. He started the Volvo and pressed a button to raise the top. The car did the rest. He turned on the air conditioning and pointed all the vents towards Mardie in the backseat.

"How long will it take?" she asked as Pfot pulled away from the curb.

"Only thirty minutes or so," Pfot answered. "With the roads repaired the ride's as smooth as a cream pie."

"Remember when it used to take four hours?"

Pfot nodded.

"My bony arse will never forget," he replied. Then he blushed. "Sorry if that was a bit too candid, Miss Mardie."

"Nonsense, Pfot," Mardie told him. "My tush has the same memories."

Pfot chuckled. Where Mili was elegant and formal, her sister Mardie was down-to-earth and silly. A nice team-up for twins. As long as one remembered which sister one was addressing.

Pfot cruised through New Babylon heading for the freeway that connected the capital to the north country and the Ben-Yehuda Kibbutz. The initial scenery was Hellish scrub and sage brush, but before long it yielded to the massive new agricultural efforts of the kibbutzniks. There were vineyards, citrus and nut trees, and hundreds of thousands of acres of garden vegetables, wheat, corn, and soy. And tobacco.

Sriracha was not the only smoker in Hell. A lot of people liked to puff away. And why not? Cigarettes were only twenty-five cents a pack.

All kinds of recreational substances were popular down here, including Alice B. Toklas's brownies. One could only get them, however, if one attended a reading by her partner Gertrude Stein and that stopped a lot of would-be fans. Stein's books were actually quite well-written. It was her personality that was a bit trying. Didn't matter to Mardie. She was a regular and ate her fill of brownies every time she went to see the famous author. Made for a very pleasant evening and a slow, relaxed walk home.

"I am supposing that Mrs. Mili wants you to get involved in her new case?" Pfot asked Mardie. Hell's demon network was sizzling with the latest gossip about Moshe Dayan's bone farm.

"She does indeed, dear Pfot," Mardie answered.

"If the demons are correct," Pfot replied, "it's a genuine mystery of mayhem and murder."

"Pfot," Mardie replied in a sarcastic tone. "Between your demon connections and lovely Nancy at the kibbutz, you are likely more informed of what's going on in Hell than my brother-in-law."

Pfot snorted and laughed, pleased that Mardie had such a high opinion of his sources.

"Of course, it's also true," Mardie went on, "that demons, devils, geists, sprites, and fairies aren't always truthful. *And* maybe you and Nancy don't set aside much time for talking. All in all, perhaps I exaggerate the breadth of your knowledge, Mr. Pfotenhauer." Mardie paused, then finished up. "Now, tell me exactly what you *do* know."

Pfot grinned.

"As best as I can report, Miss Mardie, General Dayan's pet project—his archaeological dig next to the kibbutz—has turned out to be a lost community. He thinks it was settled by Mormons a long time ago. It was apparently a good-sized town and successful despite being located in a barren unknown corner of Hell. Then for reasons unknown, the settlement was attacked and all the inhabitants were slaughtered. Moshe found mass burials yesterday and asked Mili to examine them. She ruled that the location was indeed a sizeable death pit and opened a case to discover who was murdered and by whom. At which point she called you up and asked for your help."

"Into the thick of it again," Mardie said, not entirely happy with the idea of working in a graveyard. "Some demons down here must be quaking in their boots about now, I would guess.

Those Mormons may have turned to bones and been lost to eternity, but any of the fallen angels who have knowledge, or worse, *complicity* in the town's massacre, will be tracked down by Mili."

Mardie shook her head thinking about it. There was a myriad of reasons she had always been so glad that she was not a demon. Having secret knowledge and being hunted down for it by Mili Wickett was perhaps the most telling one of all.

Mili and Moshe were at the excavation studying the baulks created by the new trench. Both walls were slices of orange clay packed with crushed bones and fragments. Mili wiped the perspiration from her face with a handkerchief and took a swallow of water from her canteen.

Moshe had a large sketch pad and was drawing the layers of soil and clay that he observed. He was wearing only khaki shorts and leather boots. Mili was wearing shorts and her halter top, and she had put on a pair of boots as well. She stared at the stratigraphy revealed by the baulk walls.

She mostly saw bones, but there was an obvious layer of black and gray ash sitting directly on top of the mass burial ground. The town had been burned down *after* all of its citizens had been slaughtered. To destroy the evidence? Or just to add one final wicked touch to the crime? Mili spotted something glittering in the clay. She carefully extracted a gold cross and held it up for Moshe to see.

"Do Mormons wear crosses?" she asked.

"No," Dayan answered. "They don't. They consider themselves Christians, but for them the cross is the symbol of Jesus's death. They prefer to confess Christ's resurrection and therefore refrain from wearing crosses or crucifixes."

Mili looked at Moshe.

"So, this was probably worn by a Christian vigilante?" she asked.

"Who was apparently killed and buried with the ones he helped murder," Moshe concluded.

Mili nodded and kept scratching here and there in the bone-infested clay. She immediately found another piece of gold jewelry. Hanging from a gold chain was a golden Star of David. She dangled it on its chain and called to Moshe again. He turned and looked.

He stared at the Star of David and frowned.

"A Magen David," he muttered using the Hebrew name for the symbol.

"Your thoughts?" Mili asked.

Moshe shook his head and remained silent. He stared at the star trying to sort out what had happened here. He spoke at last.

"Everyone must have really hated whoever lived in this town," he finally said. "Christians, Jews, and who knows who else ganged up together to wipe this Mormon settlement off the face of Hell."

Mili felt the weight of Moshe's point. It wasn't presented with Scotland Yard finesse, but its obvious truth was powerful and depressing. What had the Mormons done in this town in the middle of nowhere to cause folks in Hell to arm themselves and expunge every last soul in this place?

* * *

Moshe looked up and saw Mardie standing in her shorts and halter at the top of the baulk. His single eye went into overdrive appreciating everything that Mardie Wickett was displaying. Mili noticed and grinned.

"If you'd worn anything less, Sis, Moshe would be experiencing cardiac arrest."

Mardie grinned and Moshe chuckled.

"I think the old boy can handle it," Mardie remarked.

"Part of the old boy can," Moshe shot back. "But maybe not the heart."

At that the sisters and the dig-meister all laughed.

"Come down," Mili told her sister.

"Not on your life," Mardie replied. "I timed this so Pfot would get me here at lunch time." Mardie looked at her wristwatch. "And here I am right on the button. Time to eat?"

"We usually just grab a bite here at the site," Moshe responded. "However, in honor of your arrival we'll shower up and enjoy a repast at the dining hall."

"Did you bring any other clothes?" Mili asked her twin. "After we eat, we're coming back here again."

Mardie shook her head.

"I'm not. I had hallucinations about this work," she answered. "I'm not digging anywhere that's full of human bones."

Moshe smiled and climbed out of the trench. He gave Mardie a wave and walked off to shower and change.

Mili used the ladder Moshe had placed against one of the baulks and climbed up to stand next to Mardie.

"Mardie, this used to be a town full of folks," she began. "At some point a large group of Hell's residents arrived here and killed every last resident." Mili's voice grew more urgent. "And the evil doers who did that are not gone. *They are here in Hell.* We are going to bring them to justice. You and me. I need you to take this very seriously. *Capisce?*"

"Anything but bones."

Mili was visibly relieved.

"All right. We can do that. No bones. You can help track down the humans and the demons responsible for this massacre."

"Fine," Mardie said. "You can count on me."

"Done. Let's go eat."

"Okay. I'm sitting next to Moshe."

CHAPTER FOUR

Moshe, Mardie, and Mili sat together in a quiet corner of the kibbutz dining hall. This time of day most residents were at their jobs and only mothers and caregivers of small children were dining.

Mardie noticed.

"Lots of kids here now," she commented.

Moshe nodded.

"The kibbutz has some thirty thousand residents now and at any given time about a thousand women are pregnant."

Mili thought about that. She herself had birthed three children in Hell. Little Mardie. Sriracha. And Jesus. Now there were more boys and girls in Hell than ever. And not just at the Ben-Yehuda Kibbutz. Kids were growing up in New Babylon and throughout Hell's cities, towns, and farms. They were regular kids. Not souls condemned to damnation. So, what was their status? Were they immortal? Or would they live a normal life and die? And when they died, then what happened?

Mili was not sure that God was aware of the changes that were occurring down here, though surely some of the archangels and angels must have talked to Jehovah about the stunning upgrades to perdition over the last ten years. Maybe God knew and didn't care. Or maybe he cared and didn't know what to do. Whatever the case, sooner or later a child would die down here and then it would all be on God's lap.

Lucifer was the steward of this place, but the Almighty was responsible for it. Or was he?

Mili shook her head. Too many questions too early in the day. She had a boneyard to pick through and murderers to sort out. It was almost like being back at Scotland Yard, she thought, taking a bite of her cheese sandwich. And that felt good.

Mardie interrupted Mili's thoughts.

"Are you going to use dental records to find out who's who in the mass grave?"

"Don't see how," Mili answered. She had assumed early on that the massacre of these folks had predated widespread dental care.

"Why not?" Mardie persisted. "Folks in America were getting cavities filled as early as the 1820s."

"Really?" Mili said surprised.

"Yes. And the Utah Mormons were particularly progressive. If any of their number wound up down here, you'll find their cavities filled and their dentist records sitting pretty in Salt Lake City."

Mili nodded. She was very impressed by Mardie's information.

"Remember when you had Lucifer round up the genome data on Earth?" Mardie continued. "Trying to sort out whose bodies were being dumped on his porch?"

"Of course," Mili answered.

"Well, your husband can help us with that stuff again. Importing Mormon databases with the dental treatments administered to Mormons who may be down here."

"I will talk to him," Mili told Mardie. "If what you describe is true then I suspect that most of these residents can be identified."

"The harder part of the history," Moshe ventured, "will be discovering and finding their murderers."

Mili looked at him and nodded.

"In our favor is that the individuals who banded together to kill the Mormons are still down here carrying on. And I do know that the weapons they used had to be supplied by the demon black market. That's where I'll start my search."

"It's hard for me to believe," Dayan responded, "that Lucifer's own servants dare to violate Lucifer's ban on weapons." He poured himself more iced tea and filled the ladies' cups while he listened to Mili's reply.

"I can assure you," she said, "that anyone in Hell—demon or damned—with the money can obtain guns from demons. I personally saw a man down here shoot several residents wielding twin Colt revolvers. They were identical to the ones used to kill many of the people in the dig burial. Mardie herself got shot with a long-range rifle."

Mardie caught Moshe's eye.

"My sister is neglecting to mention that *we* were both supplied with two-shot Derringers by demons as well. Small pistols used in the old American West. Easily secreted in pockets and purses. We used ours to send an infamous serial killer to his hereafter."

"To Hell?" Moshe asked stunned.

"Yes," Mili replied. "Afterwards we tracked him down here and made sure that he disappeared a second time. That time for good. Which is exactly what's going to happen to the men and demons who orchestrated the mass murders here."

Moshe arched an eyebrow. Over his eye. He was seriously concerned.

"Would such a 'disappearance' be carried out with Lucifer's approval?" he asked. "Or with God's for that matter?"

"Questions for later," Mili answered somewhat brusquely.

Which, of course, made Dayan suppose that the answer to both of his questions was no. He drank his iced tea and bided his time.

He knew how to do that. Once upon a time he'd been a spy patiently keeping watch over the Syrians from the Golan Heights back when. Of course, he did get his eye shot out. Biding one's time had its limits.

"Moshe?" Mili asked. "How would you feel about helping us find the demons who sourced the weapons for the massacre? You and Ben-Gurion already network extensively with them regarding supplies for the kibbutz needs and to transport the produce that you grow. Would you perhaps be willing to enquire how to go about obtaining the same kinds of weapons that killed the Mormons? I suspect that the demons who supplied the Colt six-shooters that were used to wipe out the Mormon settlement could find similar weapons again."

Moshe looked troubled.

"But who would want *old* weapons?" he asked.

"Not old," Mili corrected him. "*New*. Specimens freshly made in, say, 1880."

"But how would that be possible?"

"By demons traveling back in time to the Old West and buying them." Mili eyed Moshe. "Trust me," she told him. "It can be done."

"But why not just acquire *modern* weapons?" Moshe asked. "Israel makes pistols and automatic weapons that are second to none."

Mili shook her head impatiently.

"It is important to buy the same weapons from the same suppliers who armed the killers that massacred the Latter-Day Saints."

"If they're still in the business," Moshe countered, "they're very likely no longer sourcing what are now antique weapons."

"Wrong. Remember the ambush I told you about? It happened only a few years ago and the men who died were shot to death by the killer's *new* Colt revolvers. May I also remind you that Mardie and I were both supplied with brand-new antique Derringers?"

Moshe nodded defeated.

"I will initiate contact with the demons we work with," Moshe said. "I will ask specifically how to acquire newly manufactured vintage Winchester rifles and Colt revolvers and see where it leads."

"You are so brave," Mardie told Moshe putting her hand on his forearm.

Moshe smiled.

"Ah, but it's not my bravery that draws you to me, is it, lass?" he teased.

Mardie blushed, but recovered quickly.

"What else would it be?" she teased him back. "It's not your bone field. And it's not the spooky old stuff you've crammed into your flat." Mardie gazed at him with her big blue eyes. "What else could it be?"

Dayan laughed.

"All right," he said. "Since your sister Mili is present we shall leave it at bravery."

Mili rolled her eyes.

Mardie squeezed Moshe's arm and smiled her sultriest sultry smile.

* * *

Showering a second time at the end of the workday, Mili made sure that the fine grains of clay raised by working in the dig were brushed from beneath her fingernails, washed out of her hair, and removed from every crevice exposed to their tenacious grip. She hated clay.

It was fine for pottery and school kid's art, but a land full of clay was not the kind of place she would have expected Mormons to settle. Why had they chosen this spot in Hell? For that matter, why had the Jews who founded this kibbutz decided to stake *their* futures in this location? That question she could get answered. The Mormon choice was yet one more mystery to be solved.

Mili stood under the hot water and let it relax her shoulders and back. She'd spent most of the afternoon on her knees huddled over bone pieces excavated from the clay soil. She had pried and pulled out a heap of skeletal material while an Udi from the kibbutz tried to match pieces to several skeletons being assembled up top next to the trench. By the end of the workday, six different skeletons were being filled out. Four adults and two children.

The attackers had killed children. Mili felt furious observing the sight of the small skeletons being assembled from the bones of little girls and boys. Murdering a child was always an unforgivable crime. It was an act of depravity for which there was never a justification. Mili shook her head, upset. She would find the killers of these children. She swore it on their bones.

Mili stepped out of the shower and towel-dried her hair. Her blonde hair was fine, but plentiful, and she rubbed vigorously. She'd call Lucifer as soon as she finished and ask if he'd round up the kids and meet for dinner. Little Mardie could bring Arie, her sweet kibbutz boyfriend. Sriracha could light up this and that entertaining his many young admirers. Jesus could just be Jesus, walking around smiling beatifically. And she and Lucifer could spend time together at dinner catching up on the progress of her new and troubling case.

Her call to the Devil had been short. He promised to find out where the children were. Mili appreciated that her husband had remembered to tell her that he loved her. It did, however, come only after he told her how much he loved their family dinners at the kibbutz. Hmm. She'd remind him later that her status should be considerably higher than the fare at the dining hall. She could grant that he might be able to hug a squash or kiss a chop, but there was little else he could do with those or any other foods after those preliminaries were out of the way.

Mili put on fresh panties, pink shorts, her bra, and a sleeveless white cotton blouse. The apartment was deliciously cool because she kept the air conditioning on all the time. Spending the day excavating bones and soaking her knickers had more than earned her this reprieve from the heat. Hell was still hot no matter what changes were occurring. However, now almost everyone was able to afford air conditioning, not just supermarkets and the Devil's downtown office.

After talking to Lucifer, Mili called her sister's mobile phone. Mardie answered, her face filling up the miniature phone screen.

"Am I interrupting?" Mili asked.

"Interrupting what?" Mardie shot back.

"Where are you?" Mili asked instead of answering.

"The kibbutz library."

"Reading Hebrew books?"

"No, smartass," Mardie answered. "I've been searching the World Wide Web on my laptop."

"The internet?"

"World Wide Web."

"Arcane."

"Classic."

"Fine," Mili capitulated. "Lucifer is rounding up the kids for dinner. Can you join us?"

"Sure," Mardie replied cheerfully. "Can Moshe come? He loves Sriracha, the little dickens."

"He has already promised. Want to check and see if the Ben-Gurion's want to join us? Be sure to tell them that Lucifer and all three of our weans will be with us. Is Paula okay with the kids?"

"Oh, sure. You can't live in a kibbutz and not be okay with kids. She loves kids."

"Even ones knocked silly by teenage hormones, Zippo fingers, and saintliness?" Mili enquired.

"Ha!" Mardie exclaimed. "Variety is the spice as they say."

"Yes, but remind her that all three children will be actually sitting and eating *with us* at dinner. Whether she loves kids or not, having them surround her may necessitate her doubling up on the Prozac."

There had always been copious drugs available in Hell. Easily obtained without a prescription at any pharmacy. Much like England used to be. Drug stores back when had carried opium, heroin, cocaine, and marijuana before the pressure of greedy tax legislators interfered in the twentieth century. Now all they stocked was alcohol and tobacco. But Hell still carried on the old tradition, offering all of the legendary goods—even OTC pharmaceuticals and street crack—so Paula Ben-Gurion could easily and adequately prepare herself for an evening with the Morningstar children any way that she chose.

"So, tell me, dear one," Mili continued. "What have you been researching on the World Wide Web?"

"I figured I'd see how far I could get looking for Mormon dental records in the Latter-Day Saints' records. I signed up as a researcher and was allowed access to the documents. I was stunned to see that between 1850 and 1910 there were tens of thousands of records. Exams, diagnoses, extractions, fillings, crowns, and false teeth."

"Did you sort that a bit?" Mili asked.

"Of course. I cross referenced those files against Earthly criminal records and found close to a hundred arrest and conviction files on Mormon church believers who may well have wound up going to Hell when they died."

"We uncovered parts of children's skeletons today," Mili said.

"Children?" Mardie questioned. "What were children doing in Hell back then?"

"I don't know," Mili answered quietly. "But they were slaughtered right along with the adults."

"Oh, God," Mardie said. "I will download digitized dental records for both adults *and* children and hope to heck that some of them will match the teeth dug out of the mass burial."

"I'm impressed, Mardie," Mili said sincerely. "Nice work."

"Thanks, Sis. One way or another we're going to find out who's in the scrapyard."

Mili flinched.

"*Graveyard* if you don't mind," she said softly.

"Right. Sorry," Mardie muttered. "All we have right now is a bunch of spooky bones, Mil. Turning them into people is still on the horizon."

"How soon will you be able to download the records?"

"I'll be done this afternoon."

"Brilliant."

"Heads up though," Mardie said. "I have to think that this large of a download may alert certain parties to the fact that someone down here has a use for dental records."

"Like worried Mormon historians?" Mili gently mocked.

"More like the demon network," Mardie responded completely serious. "Who knows what and who they monitor? The kibbutz links are not secure. You might even have the same demons who supplied pistols to the vigilante mob *already* worried about what Moshe is finding on the dig."

Mili felt herself shiver. Her sister's suspicions might well be true. The best prevention in Hell was snooping. Or killing. She'd seen enough guns and murders in the last few years to know that spies were everywhere and betrayals were possible any time. Mili shivered again. She said goodbye to Mardie and pressed the *Off* button on her iPhone. Then she pulled out the Derringer pistol she had tucked in her purse. It was silver-plated with a pearl handle. She checked to see that both chambers were loaded.

She vividly remembered firing bullets from the pistol into Jack the Ripper's face. She had no regrets. She'd do it again as often as necessary to protect her family, her sister, or herself. She wondered if it was true that a person who lived by the gun died by the gun to paraphrase Jesus's famous warning. Didn't matter. As long as she got her lived-by-the-gun shots in first.

CHAPTER FIVE

The dining hall looked like a school cafeteria with long tables and folding chairs. The kitchen was at the far end of the hall. There was a buffet service with rails for trays and a long row of food stalls to choose from.

Lucifer led his family to the buffet and went first. He held Jesus's hand and pointed at the available dishes. Jesus opted for baked macaroni and cheese and a big spoonful of mashed potatoes sprinkled with paprika. Mili followed with Sriracha. Her ten-year-old pushed his own food tray. Partly to feel big. Partly to make sure his mother didn't put anything on it that he didn't want. He took two pieces of pepperoni pizza which he would roll up like cigars and eat end to end.

Little Mardie and her boyfriend put their selections on a shared tray which Arie carried. They ditched the line early and went to sit with some kibbutz friends. Mili smiled as the two teenagers walked past her. They looked so happy.

She looked down at Sriracha's food selections.

"Do you want any salad?" she asked.

"I don't eat green food," he answered.

"What about some carrot slices with ranch dressing for dipping?"

"I don't eat orange food," he replied.

Mili made a little salad for herself. Lettuce, tomatoes, and avocado slices. She took a breast of roast chicken and some broiled farm salmon.

"Do you want a piece of chicken?" she asked Sriracha.

He shook his head.

"And no fish," he added.

"Lamb?"

"I don't eat babies," Sriracha said.

"Potatoes?"

"No."

Mardie took a slice of lamb for herself and cut open a baked potato. She added salt but no butter. Actually, there was no butter. The kibbutz was kosher. Dairy was not served with meat.

"May I have some dessert?" Sriracha asked. "Maybe plain old vanilla cake?"

"You can come back," Mili told him. "You have to eat your pizza first."

Lucifer led everyone to a table large enough for his family, as well as Mardie and Moshe and David and Paula Ben-Gurion. All the women were wearing shorts or slacks and cotton blouses. The men and boys were wearing black slacks and short sleeve white shirts. Training for their future duties in the Israeli Knesset. Though how a person down here could be chosen to serve in the Hebrew government was untested as of yet. But Mili was convinced that the day would surely come. If the kibbutz had managed to bring about blue skies in Hell, how hard could it be to get elected to Parliament?

After everyone had shared small talk about their day's activities all attention focused on Moshe's Mormon dig. Everyone was fascinated with his and Mili's latest news. However, as the discussions got more graphic, Mili invited Sriracha to run off and fetch a piece of cake. Jesus climbed onto Mili's lap and leaned against her chest. In moments, the littlest angel was asleep.

Moshe passed around a slideshow of the dig progress on his mobile phone. Oh, my! seemed to be the comment of choice when folks saw the bone shots. One picture showed Mili posing against one of the baulk walls. Mili and bones. Bones packed so tight there was hardly any clay to bind the lot.

"How large is the burial site?" David Ben-Gurion asked.

"We think about ten meters square and two meters deep," Dayan answered. "That probably equates to somewhere between eighty and a hundred bodies. Time has stripped the bones and gravity has crushed them together, so there might be more."

"Who have you unearthed so far?" Paula Ben-Gurion asked.

"Two men, two women, and two children," Moshe answered. This caused a distinct stir of unease among the diners.

Lucifer spoke up.

"They *can't* be children, Moshe."

"Just reading the bones, sir," Dayan answered carefully.

Satan shook his head and responded again.

"I'll grant that for some reason this obscure settlement was able to somehow safeguard its existence—even from my awareness—but never in the history of Hell has a child been damned. God would never allow it and I would never overlook it. No child has ever received a Hellion body. The skeletons may belong to small or even deformed adults," the Devil suggested. "But I guarantee that after you study them and ascertain the ages at death, *none of them* will be skeletons of children."

Moshe bowed his head respectfully.

David Ben-Gurion asked another question.

"So how large do you think the town's population was?"

"A hundred at most, assuming that all the residents were massacred."

"And those souls are lost to history?"

"Not actually," Moshe answered slowly. "Mardie believes that most of the deceased, if not all, can be identified through dental records maintained by the Mormon church in Utah. Like police procedures in use around the world, we will match names and identities with the specific work performed on the skeleton's teeth. Whether Lucifer deems this sufficient to request new Hellion bodies is his business. But he should be able to do so if he and God deem it prudent and appropriate."

Satan ate and kept his silence.

Mili spoke up.

"I have to say that any human restored to his or her identity with a replacement Hellion body would be an unimpeachable witness as to what happened to the Mormon town. Who attacked them. Who wiped out the entire settlement. Which, of course, would take the investigation to a place where the murderers could be identified and brought to justice."

Paula asked Mili the question that was on everyone's mind.

"And what happens when the guilty parties discover that they are about to be outed? Won't they try somehow to impede your excavation, and prevent the identifications?"

Mili shook her head.

"Even if the bones are somehow stolen or destroyed, we can still track down the demons who supplied the vigilantes with revolvers and identify those who used them to carry out the massacre. Bones or no bones, the guilty have no way to escape."

Paula Ben-Gurion wasn't so sure.

"What about wormholes?" she asked Mili. "I still remember the murderer from another world who used them to come and go. It's common knowledge that the vast demon black market makes extensive use of them. And we know that time bridges exist as well. You and Mardie used one to find Jack the Ripper in nineteenth-century London."

"Paula," Mili replied, "your points are valid. I don't have answers for you. All I know at this point is that we are recovering victims' skeletons and that Mardie and I will make every effort to give each person back their name and their history. Until that task is done, anything I say about who murdered the settlers and how they carried it out would just be speculation."

Lucifer spoke up again.

"I am personally disturbed by everything Moshe and Mili have uncovered in the dig," he said quietly. Everyone stopped eating and watched him. "I have no idea how or when this early Mormon settlement was established. And I can't imagine what would have caused a group of Hell's citizens to rise up and deliberately exterminate everyone living there.

"In the entire history of this place—a place filled with the worst of the worst of humankind—there has been *nothing* like this. Yet now we have undeniable evidence that a whole town of religious folk was singled out and its citizens slain."

The Devil scowled in anger.

"And now I hear that there were children here? Murdered with their mothers and fathers? Unspeakably evil even for the damned. This will not go unpunished. I promise that whatever resources are needed—human and demonic—I will find the monsters who caused this tragedy. The dead will be restored. Their murderers will be found and utterly destroyed."

Satan's face turned into a mask of hate and small flames began to dance on his sleeves. Mili reached over and took Lucifer's hand. He looked at her and the flames vanished.

"While Moshe digs and sorts," Lucifer continued, calm again, "and Mardie and Mili work to match the dental records to the dead, I will personally begin my own investigation by questioning every demon who is—or ever has been—involved in smuggling arms into Hell. I will find out who supplied the weapons used to kill the Mormon families, *and I will find out who used them*. I will work in tandem with the Wickett sisters whose goal is the same as mine. To discover the truth behind these grievous sins and punish the sinners."

"I never thought Hell could be as evil as Earth," Paula Ben-Gurion whispered.

"I agree," Moshe said. "Compared to all of the violence and misery I witnessed in the world, Hell has always seemed gentle and the people gracious. *All* of the people. And it has been ruled well by you, Lord Lucifer." Moshe complimented Satan. "You have maintained a civility and peace among the hundreds of millions of souls here that Heaven wanted nothing to do with. But now this old vendetta casts a darkness over us like a pall of death." Dayan paused and sighed. "But it does not have to spiral into a renewal of violence and killing. Count on any of us to help in any way you need to put this wickedness behind us."

There was nodding and murmured agreement. There were hugs and kisses and then everyone went separate ways. Mardie walked with Lucifer and Mili back to their kibbutz apartment. It was a large flat and Mili had invited her sister to use the guest bedroom. There was a master bedroom for Lucifer and Mili, a bedroom for Little Mardie, and a bedroom with twin beds for Sriracha and Jesus. Mili put Jesus down and turned the nightlight on. Sriracha and Little Mardie kept their own hours and no one on the kibbutz worried about them or any other young adults.

Lucifer and Mardie sat down at the kitchen table. Mili put on a pot for tea. When it had boiled and the tea had steeped, she served it black for Satan, with a bit of milk for Mardie, and with lots of cream and sugar for herself. Then she sat down and the discussions began anew.

"I have to believe there will be some pushback as your investigation goes forward," the Devil began. "The demons involved in the weapon smuggling will not want to fess up, and who knows what will happen if they do reveal the names of the buyers who destroyed the population of the Mormon town. Not one of the fallen angels came to me to report the massacre. Nor did any of the demons who supplied weapons, rode as part of the mob, or just heard the gossip that must have echoed around Hell for weeks after the secret raid."

Mili looked at Lucifer's troubled face.

"I've never heard you include demons as possible suspects before," she said.

"I was naïve," Lucifer responded bluntly. "When we encountered the Shapeshifter who raped and killed the kibbutz woman and abducted Little Mardie posing as her grandfather, my eyes were opened. Now that Moshe has revealed the tragic history of the secret Mormon settlement, we know that it had to be demons who smuggled weapons down here. Why couldn't it have been demons themselves who murdered the residents? I cannot imagine their rationale, but I will not be lulled into complacence again, Mili."

Mardie looked at her sister, and then at Lucifer.

"I want a bigger gun," she said. "*Two* bigger guns. And I know which ones." Mardie addressed Satan directly. "Where are the Colt revolvers that Jack the Ripper used?"

Lucifer frowned.

"His guns were seized and impounded."

"I want them," Mardie insisted.

"You have a pair of Derringers," Mili reminded her.

"You can have those." Mardie looked at Satan again. "Do I get the revolvers or not?" she demanded.

"Where are you going to keep them?" Lucifer asked feeling the pressure of her insistence.

"In my purse. Along with extra bullets. Make sure I get extra bullets."

Lucifer stared at Mardie and then slowly nodded.

"You could wear them in holsters on your hips," Mili teased.

Mardie snorted in derision. Then she stopped and smiled. That was actually quite something to imagine. Dressed in short shorts with the leather holsters riding her hips. Yes!

"Add holsters and do it soon," Mardie said feeling rowdy.

The Devil held up a hand as if to say enough.

"I'll have everything brought to the kibbutz tonight. You can begin practicing tomorrow."

"Practicing?" Mardie echoed. "I don't need to practice. I'll be shooting both barrels at whatever comes looking for me. Remember. Lots of bullets. *And* holsters."

Mardie left in a feisty mood. She headed out to Moshe's apartment for a nightcap. Mili and Lucifer talked together until Sriracha came home around eleven.

"You smell like smoke," his mother told Siracha. "Go brush your teeth."

Sriracha grinned and headed for the bathroom.

"No smoking in the bathroom!" Mili called after him. "And no smoking *anywhere* else in the flat, Sriracha Morningstar."

Mili looked at her husband. He was tense and irritated.

"Has this Mormon business gotten you upset?" she asked tenderly.

"Is it that obvious?" he asked.

Mili nodded.

"I don't need little flames to know when you're out of sorts, dear."

Satan grimaced and reached for Mili's hand.

"This situation is exasperating. Sad. And heartbreaking. Full of betrayal, violence, and death. The whole thing is making me feel distinctly melancholy."

"It will all work out," Mili said softly. "We have resolve. We have resources. We have each other." Mili reached up and put her hand on Lucifer's cheek. "We also have Ray Bradbury's short story on the bookshelf."

Mili rose and brought over a slim volume of stories by the master of surprise and satisfaction. Lucifer picked it up and read the title.

"Have another cup of tea," Mili told him, "and read the title story while I get Sriracha into bed. Then I'll get *you* into bed."

The Devil smiled despite himself and rose to freshen his cuppa. Then he opened the book to the first story. It was entitled "Medicine for Melancholy." He read the story, a romantic tale of the power of lovemaking to lift burdens. Lucifer was glad that Mili had thought of this. And now he was ready for her to return and fetch him to bed.

CHAPTER SIX

It took almost two weeks for Moshe to excavate all the bones in the mass grave. Mili and Mardie spent every daylight hour during that time matching Mormon dental records with the teeth recovered from the pit. In the end, many of the male skeletons were identified, but none of the women's or children's skeletons.

Mili stood on the top of the baulk where she had reassembled the excavated skeletons and they had been laid out. She was wearing taupe shorts, a Kelly-green T-shirt, and boots. Mardie had on white short shorts, a white bikini swimsuit top, cowboy boots, and her Colt six-shooters slung low across her hips in hand-tooled natural leather holsters. She actually had practiced, too, shooting the revolvers in a distant part of the citrus orchards. The guns were heavy, but the triggers were easy to pull, and the guns made very satisfying noises when the bullets exploded from their chambers.

Moshe joined Mili and Mardie matching dental records once the burials had been cleared. He personally identified the most important skeletons in the pit—Joseph Smith and his brother Hyrum. Mili stared at the remains of the two Mormon leaders. Their last actions on Earth had been to shoot down a dozen men outside the Illinois jail where they were being held. Self-defense? Or murder?

Had something similar happened here? A lot of Winchester rifles had been found in the gravesite. It appeared that the Mormons had been well-armed and had actively defended themselves, only ending their resistance when they were finally overwhelmed by the large number of vigilantes trying to gun them down. Both brothers' skulls were pierced by multiple bullet holes, and their skeletons revealed damaged and broken bones. Mili wondered if their bodies had been abused after they were dead.

She studied the skeletons that could not be identified. Eight males, eight females, and nearly two dozen children whose small statures suggested adolescents aged ten to twelve. Why weren't there more women? And why so many children roughly the same age?

Mardie walked over to her sister.

"Watch this!" she cried.

Mardie pulled the revolver from her right holster, spun it on the trigger guard, then slid it barrel first back into the empty holster.

Mili was unimpressed.

"What good is that ever going to do you?" she asked.

"Never know," Mardie responded watching Moshe walk up applauding her little trick. "Maybe impress a man who knows his guns?"

"Bravo!" Dayan cried. He took a good look at Mardie in her short shorts and hip holsters.

"Wouldn't be all that hard to imagine me wearing these with no clothes on at all, would it?" Mardie teased him and slapped the holsters with both hands.

Moshe's face turned deep red.

"I would never do that," he protested meekly.

"Well, I do it all the time!" Mardie boasted and laughed loudly.

Mili waited for her wastrel of a sister to settle down, then she drew Dayan's attention to the fact that there were so many children's skeletons of the same approximate age.

Moshe shook his head mystified.

Mardie had an opinion.

"Joseph Smith had eight wives when he died. A lot of these kids could be his."

Mili nodded. She looked at Moshe.

"Any idea how many houses were in this settlement?"

"Preliminary excavation work suggests eighty or so," he told her.

"So, homes for the Smiths and more families as well, gathered to join their Mormon leaders."

Mili, Mardie, and Moshe stood silently staring at the bones. Mili looked down at Joseph Smith's skeleton. Were some of these women his wives and mothers to his children? Very possibly. Yet that still didn't shed any light on the most basic question of this case. Why would anyone in Hell want all of them dead?

Lucifer sat at his desk in his downtown office. His quarters were spartan. No bookshelves. No cabinets. No high-tech devices. And what was there—his desk and chair and four chairs for guests—was made of asbestos. Occasionally the Devil's temper flared and this precaution saved him having to replace all the furniture every time he snapped.

Sitting across the desk from Satan was Melchior, a Shapeshifter demon in human form wearing a pinstripe business suit. He had once been a Power, a heavenly angel of majesty and beauty. He had backed Satan when the civil war erupted between the Archangel of Light's forces and Jehovah's loyal angels. Millions of angels had died. Lucifer had been cast out of Heaven along with Melchior and the rebellious angels who had not been destroyed.

He had reincarnated himself in Hell as a Shapeshifting demon, morphing his image to appear as a human. He looked a lot like the former politician turned drug merchant, John Boehner. Handsome and slick. He chose to be a weapons dealer and his ability to procure any and all kinds of weapons—guns, gas, rifles, grenades, missiles, even atomic bombs—had often decided who the ultimate winner was in conflicts like Syria, the Sudan, Libya, El Salvador, Kashmir, yadda, yadda, yadda. Of course, governments and/or rebels *only* got the weapons they could pay for, and Melchior got a huge cut of the cost of the order.

He sat facing his Lord and Master, Lucifer Morningstar. Melchior was quiet and respectful. The Devil had always known about Melchior's gun-running activities, but had never felt the need to question him. While Satan had always forbidden the sale of firearms to the citizens of Hell and Melchior had scrupulously abided with that stricture for dozens of millennia, Lucifer couldn't care less who Melchior armed on Earth.

"Melchior," the Devil said in a quiet voice. "You are the most successful arms dealer on Earth." Satan gazed at the angel with a pleasant expression. "And who knows? If you have been able to clandestinely avail yourself of the various wormholes and time bridges to the past, you might well be the greatest arms salesman in history."

Melchior nodded deeply.

Satan continued.

"I have never forgotten your loyalty and willingness to give up Paradise itself to oppose Jehovah's hatred and violence. I admired you then, Melchior. And I admire you now."

Melchior sat without moving. As beneficent as Lucifer's testimonials were, he knew that it was only at this point that the real reason for their tête-à-tête be revealed.

Lucifer leaned over his desk and made a church steeple with his fingers.

"What do you know about the massacre of Mormon townsfolk near the present Ben-Yehuda Kibbutz?"

Melchior blinked. Then he told Lucifer everything that he knew.

"I heard gossip about the existence of a Latter-Day Saints' settlement from its earliest habitation. In fact, I was approached not long after its founding by a New Babylon banker representing their leader, Joseph Smith. The Balaam said that Smith wanted to buy two dozen Winchester rifles and a lot of ammunition. He was willing to spend top dollar for the weapons and promised payment in silver. I'd already heard that demons who specialized in wealth relocation from Earth to Hell had served Mr. Smith's needs and that he was extremely wealthy.

"I asked the Balaam why the Mormons wanted to have guns in Hell which was strictly forbidden. He said that Smith and a handful of followers had been murdered in their Earthly lives. The Mormon leader was afraid that those killers would track him down in Hell and he wanted to be armed and ready. As much as I sympathized with the settlers' situation, I declined to procure the weapons."

Lucifer nodded and waited. He knew that Melchior had more to tell.

"The Mormons proceeded to build residences and a town, and they regularly received food and other supplies delivered from Earth by well-paid demons. Then maybe a decade or so after their arrival, the gossip networks came alive with reports that a group of white male vigilantes living on the frontier beyond New Babylon had made a surprise raid on the Mormons and wiped them out to the last person. I figured that it was the very reprisal that Joseph Smith had feared all along." Melchior shrugged his shoulders. "I never heard another thing."

The Devil sat back in his chair and gazed at Melchior. The demon looked back calmly.

"How long ago did this take place?"

"Almost two centuries ago."

"Who supplied the vigilantes with guns? They appear to have acquired Colt pistols."

"I do not know, my Lord. I am not the only gun dealer in Hell."

"No, you aren't," the Devil conceded. "I personally saw Colt revolvers in action down here not that long ago. The serial killer Jack the Ripper used a pair of them to cut down several men right in front of my eyes." Satan paused. "Do you know who supplied those revolvers to the Ripper?"

"I do not," Melchior answered immediately. "You might wish to check with the banker who approached me to provide Winchesters to Smith. It is rumored that he is involved in most of the illegal weapon deals in Hell."

"What's his name?"

"His demon name is Ananias Sapphira. He is a Balaam demon as I said, but in Heaven he was a Principality and had the name Ashtar. I have always found him to be honest."

Lucifer scowled.

"Honest?" he asked skeptically and arched an eyebrow.

"Maybe *reliable* is a more accurate word," Melchior quickly amended.

"Talk to him," Satan ordered. "And I will call him in as well. I want to know who provided the weapons to the Mormons *and* the vigilantes. Reach out through every other channel available to you to find out who murdered the Mormons and their families."

Melchior sat silently staring at Satan.

"Help me," the Devil told him.

Melchior nodded.

"One last question," Lucifer told him. "Back when, did you ever hear that the Mormons were bearing children down here?"

Melchior shook his head.

"No," he answered. "The common belief in Hell had always been that pregnancies and births could not happen here until you and Mrs. Morningstar proved it wrong."

"Well, apparently the Mormons down here also figured out how to have babies. Children's skeletons have been uncovered. Shot to death by the vigilantes." Satan scowled deeply. "Find me the arms dealer who sold them guns."

* * *

Lucifer called in the banker Ananias Sapphira. The tall, slim demon looked elegant in a black Armani suit and behaved with calm dignity. He readily admitted that he had arranged Joseph Smith's purchase of guns, but he proclaimed innocence in regard to servicing the vigilantes' quest for handguns.

The banker told Lucifer that the illegal weapons' transaction with the Mormons had been executed by a wildcat dealer. An extremely clever one who operated through shell companies and silent partners. How had the Latter-Day Saints learned about him? The banker didn't know. However, they had managed to get in touch, the Mormons had successfully obtained and used the Winchester rifles that the mystery gunrunner had supplied.

Satan was stumped. Thank God that his wife was a much better detective than he was. Oh sure, he'd found out how the Mormons had gotten weapons to defend themselves, but that was all. Mili would have to track down the so-called wildcat who was operating invisibly in Hell's unlawful arms trade, providing forbidden weapons to buyers down here. And he still didn't have any idea who had supplied the Colt revolvers to the vigilante mob.

Within the Devil's power, however, was his ability to appeal to God to replace Joseph Smith's Hellion body. He believed Smith could provide eyewitness testimony about who had attacked his Mormon town. He might even know the ringleaders and the men they had recruited. On the other hand, nothing but trouble had ever followed Smith. First in New York. Then in Illinois. And last of all in Hell itself. Sure, the underworld was full of troublemakers, but this fellow seemed to have the knack of turning people against him time after time. Did Lucifer really need to have him around right now?

He called Mili. She and Mardie were finishing up with the identifications of the excavated skeletons.

"Hello, love," Mili said looking at Lucifer's face on the phone screen.

"Hi," he replied a bit sadly.

"What's wrong, honey?" Mili asked.

"Missing you. Plus, this whole Mormon thing is just one long betrayal of Hell's rules. *My* rules."

"I'm so sorry," Mili sympathized. "Mardie and I and the kids will be back by dinner tonight. I miss you."

"Thank goodness. I am not much of a bachelor anymore. And apparently not very respected as a leader either."

"Nonsense. Any demons who broke the law will be disciplined. And note, they were arming men and *not* other demons. I'll see you tonight."

Satan nodded, but didn't find a lot of solace in the fact that demons weren't shooting anyone yet. They had smuggled down guns that had been used to slaughter a whole settlement of men, women, and children. And for what? Money. Filthy lucre. Just pathetic. At least when he'd rebelled against God it had been based on unselfish principles. Angels had died trying to do away with a wrathful, judgmental deity. Not for silver or gold. But for love. Where had those idealistic angels gone? Obviously, some of them had decided on gun-running. Who knew what the rest of the fallen angels were up to? Well, actually he did. Bribery. Lying. Smuggling. Stealing. Murder.

Lucifer felt embarrassed and humiliated. He felt like a two-bit tyrant whose once loyal friends and comrades had become ensnared by greed. It made him angry to think about it. Angry enough to think seriously of executing every arms dealer and dishonest banker in Hell. Would he feel better if they were dead? There was only one way to find out.

CHAPTER SEVEN

Lucifer received a second visit from Melchior the weapons dealer. He returned to report on his enquiries into which party had supplied Colt revolvers to the vigilantes.

"You have news for me?" Lucifer asked without any greetings or niceties. Melchior stood in front of the desk of Hell's master.

"I do, my Lord. I personally spoke face-to-face with every demon who deals in guns. Virtually all of them were very adamant that they *only* sold weapons to people on Earth. One demon, however, was distinctly uncomfortable when I questioned him about the Colt revolvers sold to the Hellions who shot down the inhabitants of the Mormon town."

The Devil nodded and waited.

"The demon's name is Eilers. He takes the form of a medieval devil from Bavaria. He was a Seraphim in Heaven."

"So, he sang in Heaven, but sells guns down here?" Lucifer asked, his voice tense.

"He sings down here as well. He does chorus work for the Baptists in their Biblical reenactment shows. However, he actually uses that gad-about theater time as a subterfuge to sell weapons. He is also supporting a serious cocaine habit."

"He told you all this?" Satan asked, surprised at Eilers's candor.

"Yes. He denied that he was the demon who arranged the delivery of the weapons to the mob who killed the Mormons, but he said he did hear of the deal when it went down. Two dozen Colt .44 US Army-style six-shooters were ordered. The handguns were all paid for with American silver dollars at one thousand dollars per. He said there was no intermediate banker."

"He told you those exact details?"

"Yes," Melchior replied. "But he was very defensive. He claims that he serves large-volume purchasers. He said that he would not take kindly being blamed for the small weapon sale you are investigating."

Satan scowled. Disrespect *and* a veiled threat?

"I'll summon him," Lucifer responded. "You may wish to find some other place in the Universe to visit for a while."

Melchior bowed. Then he stood and left.

Lucifer sent two Samn demons to find Eilers. Time to see what cards the arms dealer was holding.

* * *

Mardie and Mili were squatting, examining a child's skeletal remains. It was laid out with the rest of the reassembled skeletons. It was a sobering sight. Mili had a tape measure in hand and was measuring the pelvis of the young child's skeleton.

"A mature female's pelvis is bigger than a male," she told Mardie. "During puberty it is enlarged and rounded to allow a baby to pass through during the birth process. None of these small skeletons show evidence of that maturation. That means we can't use them to determine the sex of these children."

"Are you saying that you can't tell if these are boys or girls?" Mardie asked.

"Not with just a visual exam, I'm afraid," Mili replied. "However, DNA samples can immediately determine the sexes of all of the murdered children."

Mardie stood up and flexed her legs.

"You have a lab and technicians available at the New Babylon Hospital," she told her sister. "Let's gather the bones you need and take them with us when we head back." Mardie paused and looked at Mili. "Which is tonight, right?"

"Yes, and we'll do dinner at your house if that's okay. I want to finish some last observations here before I have Moshe store the bones."

"I'm skipping dinner," Mardie replied. "I miss Bowles."

Mili craned her neck and looked up at Mardie.

"Well, I have to say I'm glad to hear that. I like Bowles."

"Me, too," Mardie answered. "Very much."

"And what about Moshe?"

"He's fun. I love to have coffee and conversation with him."

"And?"

"And that's all you'll get out of me."

"No kiss and tell?"

"No anything and tell."

Mili grinned and went back to her skeleton.

Mardie turned, hearing someone approach. Crunchy steps on the clay soil alerted her to the visitor. It was a green demon no more than three feet tall. He was naked except for a green thong the same color as his skin. He was holding a small automatic weapon at his side. Maybe an Israeli Uzi. About the right size considering his height. She'd run into this kind of demon before, most memorably doing grunt work at a temporary morgue set up at a meat packing plant for the corpses that had been systematically dumped on Lucifer's front porch.

"May I help you?" Mardie called out as the demon approached. Mili stood up and stepped next to her twin.

"Pardon the interruption ladies," the demon said. He had a pleasant alto speaking voice.

"Why are you carrying a weapon?" Mili challenged him. "It is forbidden to have weapons in Hell."

"It is an incentive for you to come with me peacefully," the demon answered.

"Who are you?" Mardie asked, instantly upset.

"My name is Eilers and you are my protection," he answered smoothly. "Lord Lucifer has asked to see me regarding a shipment of handguns provided to certain residents down here more than two hundred years ago. Apparently, they were used to turn the inhabitants of a Mormon town into the skeletons you've laid out."

"Don't be a smartass," Mili warned. "Why are you here?"

"I thought I had just explained that quite reasonably," the demon answered maintaining a polite voice. "I am taking you and your sister hostage until I am granted safe passage out of Hell by your husband, Mrs. Morningstar."

Mili scowled furiously.

"It is to be assumed then that *you* were the dealer who provided the guns to whoever murdered these people?"

"You don't have to assume," the green demon replied. "I will tell you straight out. When I was asked to take the order, I spoke to the men who made no secret of the fact that they were planning to raid and destroy this settlement." The demon assumed a benevolent expression. "I asked them why they would want to do such a thing. The reason they gave shook me right down to my toes. I willingly agreed to fill their order then and there, and right up to this very moment—standing right here beside the victims' remains—I am proud that I did."

Those were the last words the demon spoke. Mardie whipped out both of her Colt six-shooters and pulled the triggers again and again. Several bullets penetrated the demon's chest and stomach. He looked amazed and then cried out in grievous pain collapsing on the ground. Blood flowed freely from his multiple wounds and he did not move. Mili bent close and heard the dying demon exhale a long last breath. In an instant, the fallen angel reverted to its original Seraphim shape. A small, perfectly formed, pink-bottomed little blonde cherub lay dead, shot to pieces and still bleeding.

Mili turned to Mardie.

"Thank you. I have no idea how that bastard thought he could use us to guarantee his escape. But his plan ran into a glitch. You."

Mardie emptied the brass casings from her guns. Then she pulled fresh bullets from the leather loops on her holster belt and loaded them. Mili watched as Moshe and a handful of people who'd heard the shots came running up armed with clubs, pitchforks, and knives.

"When did you learn those fast-draw moves?" Mili asked Mardie, impressed by the lightning response her sister had had to the would-be kidnapper.

"After I got tired of the twirly whirly thing," Mardie answered. She gave both Colts simultaneous twirls and dropped them barrel first into her holsters.

"Who is that?" Moshe asked looking at the dead angel on the ground.

"It was the arms dealer who supplied the Colt revolvers to the mob that killed this town,"

Mardie answered. "Lucifer got wind that it was him and summoned him for a heart to heart."

Mili continued the story.

"The bastard thought he could hold us hostage in return for my husband's promise of free passage out of Hell. Wrong. It's doubtful whether Lucifer would have shot the asshole, but Mardie did."

Everyone stared at the little angel. How odd that something so beautiful had hidden itself away as a fat green toad for so many eons. Mili realized that she had to let Satan know what had just happened.

She took out her mobile phone and called him even as Dayan told the folks who had followed him to fetch some blocks of ice from the kibbutz and place them in a nearby work shed. He'd keep the body cold until Lucifer wanted it burned or buried.

Mili tugged at Moshe's arm before he left. He looked at her.

"The demon told us that he asked the vigilantes why they wanted to destroy the settlement. They told him. Whatever reason they gave persuaded them as to the righteous of their cause. So much so, that he claimed he remained pleased to this very day that he had procured the guns for them to carry out the mass murders."

"He didn't reveal their reason?" Moshe asked.

"No," Mili answered. "It would have been worth hearing I'm sure. But he carried that information into oblivion along with Mardie's bullets."

"Maybe he was just blowing smoke up his own ass," Dayan suggested rudely.

"Maybe he was," Mili agreed looking down at the naked body of the deceased angel. "And maybe he wasn't."

* * *

Mili reached Lucifer on his mobile phone while he was catching up on work at his New Babylon office. She described Eilers and his fateful encounter with Mardie and her revolvers.

"I am sorry that Eilers took it upon himself to barter for his escape by trying to cart you and Mardie off," the Devil told his wife. "Makes me totally enraged."

"Not your fault, love. I think his fear of being exposed and punished drove him mad."

Lucifer thought about that for a moment. Then went on.

"His heavenly name was Flexor. He was a Seraphim who sang so hard you could see his vocal cords vibrate. He was quite devoted to singing praises to God until Jehovah wrenched away anyone else's right to rule by binding the other aspects of Elohim in perpetuity."

Mili watched her husband shake his head sadly.

"Do you want me to send a picture?"

"No, no, no. Whatever remains has been tainted by Flexor's later devotion to money and his willing collusion with the killers who murdered the Mormons. I'll remember him as the little chap singing his heart out before Elohim's crystal throne."

"God sits on a throne of crystal?" Mili gasped imaging it.

"Elohim never stinted on the decor, I'll tell you that," the Devil commented. "Jehovah himself likes to go first cabin, too. Even when he planned Jesus's Earthly life and mission, he had him grow up in a rich man's home with everything in abundance. His 'father' Joseph was the lead building contractor working on the expansion of Sebaste, a Roman city in Galilee that had already been lavished with gorgeous architecture by Israel's conqueror General Pompey. And after him by Herod the Great who had received the city as a gift from Emperor Augustus. Everything and everyone associated with that town has always been rich, rich, rich."

"Then Jehovah must have been pretty pissed off when the Romans leveled his gold-and- marble temple in Jerusalem."

"Not as pissed off as he already was at the Jews. He thought they were lax. Thought they were wishy washy. He let them know that a day of judgment and destruction was coming. And by the time it came at the hands of the Roman Empire, Jehovah didn't have many Jewish admirers left."

"How can you stand dealing with him?" Mili asked.

"Who said I could stand it?" Satan grimaced. "I *hate* having to ask him for Hellion replacements. Which I now have to effin do yet again in order to get Joseph and Hyrum Smith to sit down with me and name their town's attackers."

"You're sure you want to do that?" Mili asked.

"I'm sure I *don't* want to do that," the Devil grumped. "But I like even less knowing that a vigilante force decided to murder a town full of Mormons and managed to hide it from me for two centuries smugly believing that they got away with it."

Mili had another thought.

"Before you ask God to bring Joseph and Hyrum back, consider that they will likely insist on having all their wives and children restored as well. And I have no idea how you're going to explain to Jehovah the presence of dead children in Hell."

"What other options do I have?" Satan asked.

"Maybe the best option is to have another face-to-face with the banker, Ananias Sapphira. Despite his denial of details, I would wager that he is a walking Wikipedia about everyone who has ever purchased weapons from the gun dealers in Hell. Buyers on Earth won't know or care about what he tells you. But any sellers and buyers down here will have a lot to worry about."

Lucifer held his hand up and said he had to take an incoming call. Only his family and his closest staffers had his mobile number. The screen went dark and silent on Mili's side. Lucifer looked at the face of his new caller and listened. He frowned and nodded. Then without speaking anything at all he hung up and returned to Mili.

"It was the night supervisor at my office," he said identifying the interrupting caller. "He just got word that the banker Ananias Sapphira was murdered in a New Babylon restaurant just minutes ago."

Mili frowned.

"A timely coincidence," she remarked. "Any details?"

"Only one," Lucifer responded. "But you'll love it. A man dressed in a black suit and a bolo and string tie entered the restaurant, walked right up to Sapphira's table, and shot him point-blank in the chest with a Colt .44 revolver."

"Dear God!"

"Everything he knew and might have told us is lost," Lucifer said unhappily. "You know there are no restorations for fallen angels."

Mili nodded.

"Yes," she answered. "But this blatant murder just confirms that there are indeed individuals living in New Babylon who know as much or more about the slaughter of the Mormons than your dead banker did. *And* may well have killed him off just now to keep that specific information unspoken."

"Whoever that was may wonder what exactly you have learned about all of this. Be extra careful, love."

"You know I won't stop, though, right?" Mili asked.

"Do Scotland Yard inspectors shit in the woods?" Lucifer responded, and managed a small chuckle. Of course, they did. But if it was Mili, he was sure that it wouldn't smell.

CHAPTER EIGHT

Mardie sat on a barstool at the Good News Club. Bowles was tending bar and popping out to take care of customers sitting at tables. It gave him a chance to look at Mardie's legs, long and tan, with the hem of her white shift starting at her upper thigh. She had on five-inch strap-back stilettos and her sapphire-colored blouse was unbuttoned three buttons down.

She caught him looking and winked. He whispered "I love you" every time he passed her.

Bowles had, of course, heard the endless gossip here at the club about Mardie and Mili's new case. A terrible case. The massacre of an entire community. A demon banker being shot to death. And hair-raising tales of a gunrunner who asked Mardie at gunpoint to cooperate and received twelve answers from her twin Colt revolvers.

Mardie was waiting for Mili to join her at the Good News Club. She and Mili had arrived back in New Babylon late in the afternoon. Her twin was at the city hospital attending to the body of the murdered banker, Ananias Sapphira. Mili had asked Mardie to go with her earlier when they were finishing tea and pastries in Mardie's lovely kitchen. Maple cupboards. Iron stove. Old-fashioned ice box.

"No," Mardie told her. Firmly.

Mili frowned.

"I need the powers of your observation."

"No."

"Why are you being stubborn?"

"Want some more tea?" Mardie asked changing the subject.

Mili nodded and pushed her cup and saucer towards her sister. Mardie filled it up with hot Twinings ginger tea. Then she got up and refilled the pastry plate with shortbread biscuits. Mili sipped at her fresh tea and ate a half dozen cookies.

"I don't enjoy being around dead bodies," Mardie finally said.

"No one does, dear," Mili replied, adding lots of cream and several spoons of sugar to her tea.

"*You* do," Mardie answered taking exception.

"Only in the context of doing my job," Mili protested.

"Of course," Mardie said. "Just like you only take interest in cookies in the context of eating."

"I *enjoy* the cookies."

"And you *enjoy* the dead bodies." Mardie looked at her sister. "I do not."

Mili shook her head.

"This is the first male demon I've ever scheduled for an autopsy. I suspect that Lucifer would not have let it happen if he weren't preoccupied with having to go to God about Hellion bodies for the Smith brothers. He is hoping that word has not yet reached Jehovah that the Smiths were murdered two hundred years ago and that the perpetrators were never apprehended."

"Why should God care? Who in their right mind wants people to suffer damnation for eternity based on their pathetic little lives?"

"Good point, but for whatever divine small-mindedness he may possess, Jehovah may take Lucifer to the woodshed over this incident."

"So, it's *embarrassing* for Lu," Mili summed up.

"That it is."

"He'll be fine. You'll be fine. Enjoy your autopsy." Mardie stuffed an entire cookie in her mouth the way Mili did and talked while she chewed.

"I'm going to go to the Good News Club tonight and flirt with Bowles, *and* see a new Biblical reenactment."

"What is it?"

"*David and Bathsheba.*"

"Lust and adultery."

"Not the way the Baptists do it. But it might be a *little* saucy."

"May I join you when I'm finished?" Mili asked.

"Of course," Mardie replied happily. "But wash your hands after you finish with the body. At least four or five times."

Mili watched the completion of the autopsy and looked at the Colt pistol slug that had been removed from the angel's body and laid in a metal bowl. It was round rather than an elongated like a Colt .44 slug. She knew that it had been shot from a navy-style .36 Colt pistol. What struck her the most was that someone had gotten close enough to the Balaam demon Ananias Sapphira to put a bullet into his lungs.

The demon had died almost instantly in the restaurant where he'd been shot. His angelic body was tall and muscular. His organs and skeleton had revealed themselves to be virtually identical to human versions. The only odd thing was that the angel had four toes on each foot. Is that an anomaly, she had asked the surgeon performing the autopsy? He looked closely at each foot.

Right and left both had a large toe, two middle toes, and a pinky toe. They appeared to be naturally formed, he told her. They were not aberrations. The toe and foot bones were not deformed in any way. The planter surfaces were narrower than human feet, but that was because they were tailored to work with four toes instead of five. Four toes, Mili pondered. No wonder angels sang instead of danced.

Then she stopped dead and stared at the dead angel's feet. What about Lucifer's feet? He was an archangel. Yet she never noticed whether he had four toes instead of five. How did a wife of almost twenty years miss a detail like that? She was not sure that she had ever carefully observed his feet. He never went barefoot. He did not go swimming with her and the kids. He did not wear sandals. He did not walk around the bedroom before bed with his shoes and socks off. She thought she could have noticed when he got out of the shower, but she had not.

Four toes. How odd. Mili tucked that information away in the recesses of her brain until she could ask Lucifer about it. And make him take his shoes and socks off.

When Mili walked into the Good News Club, Bowles noticed her immediately. He walked over to greet her.

"Mili, it's been an age," he said graciously. "You haven't changed a bit." He took Mili's hand and planted a light kiss on top.

Mili smiled. It had been less than two weeks. He had given her a compliment to be a dear. She liked Bowles very much. And though she never said it to her sister, she was sure that the French-Moroccan gentleman was a very civilizing influence on her twin. Early on Mardie had mastered the walk and talk of a teenage slut, but as of late she had developed an elegance and an occasional coyness that was quite charming. She probably dropped all such mannerisms during sex and roared like a bear when she came, but Mili never had to witness that. The public behaviors that she *did* see pleased her. And she largely credited them to Bowles' suave example.

"And how are *you*, Bowles?"

"Better for having seen you," he said and escorted her to where Mardie was seated at the bar. Bowles had another good long look at Mardie's legs and Mili noticed their bare glamour as well. Mili took a barstool next to her sister and asked Bowles to bring her a glass of chardonnay.

"Hi, Sis," Mardie greeted her. Mili could tell she'd been here awhile. She was mellow and happy. "How did things go in the lab?" she asked Mili.

"Fine," Mili answered, still a bit miffed that Mardie had refused to accompany her. She had managed to notice the four-toe phenomenon on the snuffed angel, but who knew what else she had missed?

"How long are your legs?" she asked her sister, staring at them.

"My inseam is a thirty-six."

"My God," Mili blurted out. "Mine is a thirty-two."

"Good for a dame that grazes five foot ten," Mardie told her.

"But thirty-six? You're the same height as me." Mili was still stunned. She looked at Mardie. "You don't look short-waisted."

"No one looks at how *tall* my torso is," Mardie remarked drolly.

"Ha!" Mili laughed. She toasted Mardie with the glass of Newton unfiltered chardonnay that Bowles had just set on the bar for her. She took a sip. So nice.

"So, what discoveries did you make today?" Mardie asked. She seemed truly interested in the autopsy results.

"The banker was shot in the chest right below the second rib. Just missed his heart. The shooter got so close I imagine that the Balaam knew him. Probably told him hello. The end result of their greetings was a bullet to his insides."

"That sounds more like a mob hit in New York or London. Not Hell. It's always been safe to do anything down here," Mardie commented.

"I know. Makes me sad."

"What kind of weapon?" Mardie asked.

"Colt .36. A navy version of the army guns you have. It fires a small ball instead of a bullet."

Mardie gasped softly.

"Can you match it to any of the slugs we found in the Mormon gravesite?"

Mili stared at her sister.

"That's a brilliant question, Mardie." Mili's eyes sparkled with excitement. She reached over and took Mardie's hand. "See why I need you next to me? I'll call Moshe and have the bullets delivered to Lucifer's office. We can group them by barrel striations on the lead from whichever guns fired them. We might even be able to determine how many guns were in play during the massacre." Mili's voice dropped to a whisper. "And perhaps eventually match them to the Colt six-shooters still in the hands of those responsible for those murders."

"But let's match them without having to pull bullets out of our own bodies, all right?" Mardie responded. She was sorry that she couldn't wear her Colt revolvers to the club, but she did have her Derringer tucked inside her purse. Each of its double barrels was loaded with a bullet. Not as good as twelve bullets packed into the chambers of two Colts, but she'd make it do in a crisis. Quality, not quantity.

It had worked on Jack the Ripper, whom she had shot and killed in tandem with Mili. Granted that bastard had to be killed a second time down here in Hell, but there were a lot of helping hands at that second scenario. Jack lived by the gun, but died burned to a crisp by Samn demons who had leveled his apartment building with fire.

"Let's move to a table for the reenactment," Mili suggested, letting go of Mardie's hand.

Mardie looked towards Bowles. He immediately came over.

"Darling, can you move us to a table?" Mardie asked. "And bring a cold bottle of whatever Mili is drinking, and another one that matches mine."

"Of course," Bowles responded. "I've reserved a table a bit to the side, but with a clear view of the front of the stage. It will allow you and Mili to talk during the performance without getting dirty looks."

"Do we talk during the performances?" Mardie asked surprised.

"Yes, you do. About whatever case you're both working on, I suspect. Why should tonight be different?" Bowles winked and led the Wickett sisters to their table. He fetched the wine they asked for and put the bottles in stand-up marble coolers along with a large dish of warmed cashews.

"Bowles said we talk during all the performances," Mardie told Mili.

"Only during the scenes where there's no sex," Mili explained.

Mardie nodded.

"So, during *all* the scenes."

"Yes," Mili said filling Mardie's glass and her own. "We talk through all the performances."

CHAPTER NINE

The theater lights went dark and the sound system began to play the kind of Hollywood movie music that had been around since Cecil B. DeMille had used it to score his black-and-white *Ten Commandments* in 1923. The epic melodramatic trumpet-and-drum processional music became the standard soundtrack for every future pageant about ancient Egypt. And ancient Greece. And ancient Rome. Ancient anywhere where they drank and fought with swords.

The lights came up to reveal King David—red-haired and freckled—rendering judgments on his lavish throne. Mili looked at the handsome actor who played David. He was fair and buff. Handsome as the play was long. The real David had ruled Israel around 1000 BC and was said to have been the handsomest man in the kingdom. Maybe so. He had at least eight wives and a large number of concubines. Of course, David's numbers paled compared to his son Solomon. As king his son managed to acquire over a thousand wives and concubines. Bloody Mormons, Mardie thought. Both of them.

The actor playing David sang some song about loving the Lord more than gold and silver. Might have been true, Mili thought. She noted that he didn't sing lyrics declaring that he loved God more than women. King David had a checkered personal history that included lying, treason, murder, and with Bathsheba he was about to add adultery. Yet for all his mischief Jehovah said that David was a man after his heart. Said a lot about the God of the Bible.

By every honest calculation David should have been damned to Hell. Instead, he was in Heaven. Lucifer himself had seen him playing the harp and singing songs at one of God's celestial banquets. It also occurred to Mili that there was no divine homage to women in the scriptures where God proclaimed that a certain female was a woman after his own heart. Said that much more about the God of the Bible.

Mili leaned towards Mardie and whispered, "The dead angel in the morgue only had four toes on each foot."

Mardie frowned and turned to Mili.

"What?"

Mili held up four fingers, her thumb tucked behind her palm.

"Only four toes," she repeated.

"So what?" Mardie asked.

"Apparently it is a difference between angels and humans," Mili explained.

"I repeat. *So what?*"

"I don't know yet. But don't you think that's a surprise?"

"Who cares?" Mardie replied. "If angels had four penises I might want to know more."

Mili got up and walked back to the bar.

Bowles greeted her.

"Finished your wine already?" he asked.

"No, no, no," Mili said. "Do any demons work here in the café?"

"Aye. There's a little one that cleans up and does dishes during the dinner hour."

"Green?"

"No. Orange. Green ones are Catholic. Orange ones are Protestant."

"I saw a dead green one earlier this week. Should have checked his toes."

Bowles stared at Mili confused.

"I'm only muttering, sorry," Mili responded. "Is the chap who buses the dishes around?"

"Should be."

"Can I go to the kitchen and see him?"

Bowles shook his head.

"Let me bring him to you, ma'am. He is a demon. Nice enough as far as I can tell, but you should meet him out here where I can keep my eye on him."

"Thank you, Bowles. I only need a moment of his time."

Mili sat at the bar and watched the reenactment. David had gone to the "roof" of his palace and was looking down on a beautiful naked woman bathing in the privacy of her gardens. Mili saw that the actress was wearing a flesh-colored body stocking. Didn't hide her generous breasts and hips, however. Any more than Janet Leigh's leotard had hidden her curves in the shower scene in Hitchcock's *Psycho.*

Bowles walked up with a three-foot-tall orange demon. He was bald and naked save for a loin cloth and boots. Mili instantly liked the smiling imp.

"What's your name?" she asked.

"Pike," he answered.

"Hello, Pike," she told him. "Do call me Mili."

The demon nodded politely.

"Pike," Mili went on, "would you mind slipping your boots off and let me see your feet?"

The demon turned to Bowles who looked surprised, but he nodded to the little chap to do as the lady asked. The miniature devil sat on the floor and untied the laces of his boots, pulled them off, and shucked his grimy white socks as well. He held his feet high for Mili to inspect.

Son of a bitch, Mili thought. Four toes. Exactly like the dead Balaam. Four toes. She shook her head. Something somewhere lurking in her detective's mind was troubled by the fact that demons only had four toes on a foot.

"Thank you so much, Pike," Mili told the demon. "It was nice to meet you and thank you for your help."

"Can I put my boots back on?" he asked.

"By all means," Mili replied kindly. "Thanks again."

The demon pulled his socks and boots back on and hurried away. Bowles was watching Mili, hoping for an explanation.

She addressed him.

"Did you know that demons only have four toes on each foot, Bowles?"

"Everybody knows that," he answered.

"Well, everyone does *now*," Mili answered. "Thanks for your help." She looked at Bowles a moment, then asked, "Is there anything else unusual about angels that *some* people might not know?"

Bowles shrugged.

"Some folks may not know that there aren't many full-size female angels. There are, however, a lot of pint-sized females—fairies and sprites, nymphs and pixies—but very few large lady angels."

Mili wrinkled her forehead.

"Why have I never seen one of these smaller versions? I'd think they'd be rather easy to spot."

"Unlike regular demons," Bowles replied, "who are everywhere and have their fingers in everything, the wee angels are domestic, preferring to be married, and making it a point not to be seen."

"And they only have four toes on a foot?"

Bowles smiled and nodded.

"All angels large and small. Four toes."

Mili waved at Bowles and headed back to the table where Mardie sat absorbed by David scrubbing Bathsheba's back. Mili sat and downed her glass of wine. She refilled it. Wanted to down that too, but the fact was the things that she was discovering were new and thrilling. A bit of wine would enhance her happy feelings. Too much and it would take the edge off the excitement she was feeling. Everyone knew that Elohim had created millions of male angels. But why so few female angels? And why had so many of them been consigned to the small and cute category? Pixies, sprites, and fairies?

Mili sipped at her wine and focused on the performance. David had led Bathsheba to his bedroom and the stage lights went out. It wasn't intermission, just a bit of forbidden viewing.

Sure enough, in a minute the lights were back on and David was once again seated on his throne. Time apparently had passed. He was being informed by a servant from Bathsheba that she was pregnant. David dismissed the messenger and sent for his general Joab.

David asked Joab who Bathsheba's husband was. The general told him that his name was Uriah, one of the military commanders leading a clean-up campaign against local Canaanites. Have him relieved and sent home to spend a weekend with his wife, David ordered, hoping that the baby didn't turn out to have red hair and freckles.

Wicked man, Mili thought. Running from his sin and his responsibilities. Yet right in character for David it seemed. Get another man's wife pregnant and connive to make the man think it was his child. Slimy bastard. Mili looked at Mardie.

"Bowles said that fairies and the smaller angels are all female and like to be hidden away with a partner."

Mardie looked at Mili.

"They're all lesbians?" Mardie asked.

"No. Sorry. Wrong choice of words. Bowles said they like to be married."

"To whom? Some big lug Samn demon?" Mardie asked. "Heaven forbid."

"Apparently Heaven *hasn't* forbidden it," Mili replied. "But *who* they're marrying is the mystery, isn't it?"

The play went on, but Mili barely paid attention. Bathsheba's husband visited her, but didn't lie with her since his soldiers were unable to see their own wives. David slapped his forehead when he heard that. He ordered the man placed on the front lines of the battle and was brought word that he had been killed. David was off the hook and promptly took Bathsheba into his palace as his newest wife.

"Have you ever slept with a demon?" Mili asked her sister.

Mardie stared offended, then answered.

"Not on your life!" she said with venom in her voice. "And why are you asking me? *You're* married to one in case you forgot."

"Shut up," Mili snapped.

"What was the point of that question?" Mardie asked getting truly angry.

"I can answer it myself as you've pointed out," Mili replied. "I was just wondering if there was anything surprising about their bodies or their lovemaking."

"And?" Mardie led her on.

"In a nutshell, I don't think so. Why then aren't *other* demons having babies if they're messing with the fairies and sprites and so on? The demons certainly *have* to be capable of impregnating them. Do you remember in the Bible when angels were allowed to mingle with Earth women and had offspring with them?"

"No."

"Oh, sure you do. Genesis says that they produced a race of giants."

"I don't remember."

"Goliath was one of them. Great big chap fighting for the Philistines. Goliath's size alone caused King Saul to piss his armor. David took the giant down with his sling and that was that."

"The same David as this one?" Mardie asked and pointed at the actor sitting on David's throne.

"Yes, this one," Mili told her.

Mardie shook her head.

"So, the question still remains. Who are the little angels marrying? And why aren't they having any babies?"

"Maybe Bowles is wrong," Mardie pointed out. "I mean, when would he ever have seen any of that himself?"

Good point, Mili thought and drank some more of her wine. Somchow her sleuth instincts knew that there was a connection between the hidden lives of the little female angels, the fact that demons had no sex outlets in Hell, and that God had marked all angels with feet bearing four toes, not five. None of this had been taught in Sunday School. Not that she had attended. She was on her own, except for pestering Mardie who was now deeply absorbed as the reenactment raced towards its climax.

Mili decided that she needed fresh air. She stood up quietly. Mardie didn't even notice. She walked over to the bar. Bowles looked at her.

"Be a dear and tell Mardie that I had to leave," Mili told him. "My mind has gotten so agitated I've decided to walk back to her house."

"It would be better if I called Pfotenhauer to fetch you," Bowles suggested diplomatically.

"All right, thank you."

In ten minutes Mili was on her way to Mardie's house where she, Lucifer, and the kids were staying. She was riding in the new family Volvo with Paul Pfotenhauer at the wheel. After greeting him, Mili had fallen silent, her brain stirred up by thoughts about demons and giants, pixies and kids. She wondered if Lucifer—like other angels—had romanced women on Earth in the early days of Creation. She tried to put that thought out of her mind. But it nagged a bit. Had he perhaps remained celibate until he'd met her? No. She remembered his "professional" relationship with Cleopatra who wanted to hawk her wines in Hell. Had he had other flings or relationships?

"Pfot," she asked. "Are you aware of how demons satisfy their sexual needs?"

Pfotenhauer peeked at Mili's face in the rearview mirror.

"I don't believe that most of them have an opportunity to do so."

"But they do have urges?"

"As far as I know. But for most demons, other urges are more powerful. Usually, the one to be rich."

Mili pondered that a moment.

"Would you say that is true of human males as well?"

"Not really, ma'am," Pfot answered. "Men like sex, but they also want female companionship. Being with a caring and nurturing woman is a powerful need in and of itself."

"Why is that do you suppose?"

"My own thought is that it's because men have mothers. They are exposed to feminine love and kindness from a wee age and that impact—and the desire to experience it again—are sunk deep in the male psyche. Angels, on the other hand, were made by God. They didn't have a mother. Just a father. They may have been loved and cared for by Elohim, but they were just a brood of unwanted extras after Jehovah took control."

Mili nodded. Spot on Pfot, she thought. He completely understood the difference between the lifelong effect of having a loving mother and the emotional poverty when deprived of that special caring. It was a huge difference between Mardie and her. Even now. Not a day passed that her sister didn't long for the mother's love she never had.

"Pfot, step on it!" she suddenly blurted out. "It's urgent that I get to Mardie's house as quickly as possible."

"Yes, ma'am!" Pfot responded and put the pedal to the metal.

The moment Mili got out of the car she ran for the house and dashed into the guest bedrooms where the children had their beds. She went to Little Mardie first. She was rolled up in her blankets like a mummy. Mili carefully unrolled the covers around her daughter's feet. It was dark in the room, but she could clearly see five toes on each foot.

She checked Sriracha next. He was sprawled on top of his bed with his blankets thrown off. He smelled like smoke. Mili stood a little way away from her cigarette smoke-saturated boy and counted five toes on each foot.

She went Jesus's bed last. He liked going to bed in a cloth baby sleeper even though he was five years old. He was asleep with a smile on his face. Of course, Mili thought. She reached down and felt Jesus's right foot through his nappy. Four toes. She counted again. Four toes. She felt his left foot. Four toes. She went out and closed the door.

How the Hell had she missed the fact that while Little Mardie and Sriracha had normal human feet, Jesus had angel feet? Did it matter? She didn't know. Her children had inherited different angelic and human traits. Did *that* matter?

It was late, but Mili was not in the mood to go to bed and count Lucifer's toes. She went into the kitchen and pulled a package of chocolate ice cream bars out of the refrigerator freezer. She unwrapped one and took a bite. Vanilla ice cream dipped in a dark chocolate coating. She ate it and had another. Four toes? Five toes? Married pixies? Angels without mothers? One by one she ate the rest of the chocolate ice cream bars and sat deep in thought. Solving nothing.

CHAPTER TEN

Lucifer was at the kitchen table drinking coffee when Mili came down. She had showered and was dressed in a gray linen dress and black sandals. She gave her husband a peck on the cheek and poured herself a cup of coffee.

"Ready for a refill, love?" she asked the Devil. He nodded and she topped off his coffee. His mug had a picture of a cartoon family posing in front of a hamburger joint. "Who are they?" Mili asked.

"Characters in the best show on Earth television," Satan replied. "As perfect a bunch of misfits as could be dreamed up by mortal man. Husband wired and anxious. Wife manic about life's little pleasures. Kids truly disrespectful and mouthy. Friends easily classified as sociopaths and borderline psychopaths."

"God spare us all," Mili said and began scooping sugar into her coffee. "And the kids watch this with you?"

"Little Mardie does. We saw half a season in one sitting." Lucifer took a sip of his coffee and smiled happily. "Sriracha watched some with us when he wasn't smoking."

"Thank you for not letting him smoke in Mardie's house."

"I didn't ban him from the house," Satan replied tentatively. "Just from the living room. I think he smoked in the bathroom."

Mili groaned.

"You don't think he might be stunting his growth, do you?" she asked.

"Not down here," the Devil answered, watching her spoon sugar into her coffee. "No lung diseases, remember?" He nodded towards her cup. "No diabetes either."

Mili nodded, poured cream in her coffee, and drank standing by the table.

"You're off this early?" Lucifer asked.

"Pfot is fetching me and Mardie to check out the slugs you had sent over from Moshe's dig."

"They're waiting for you at the office in a small wooden box on my desk. It's a cool gizmo where you touch the lid and it literally pops off. Inventor of that great item is down here. Died of a stroke while he was working on a coffin constructed on the same principle."

Mili envisioned that. A pop-off casket top. Convenient for sure. She finished her coffee and put the cup in the sink.

"What are you up to today?" she asked Lucifer.

"Little Mardie has been invited to spend the weekend at the kibbutz with Arie. I told Sriracha he could go, too. He loves his friends there."

"Aye. A bunch of junior arsonists."

"They're careful. Never heard of them lighting up anything more than crumpled-up cigarette packages."

"Oh, sure," Mili replied with a sarcastic tone to her voice. "And what are you and Jesus doing?"

"You mean now that you're about to abandon him and me?"

"I'll only be gone a couple of hours. He doesn't even wake up until noon."

"Sorry," Lucifer quickly apologized. "I'll be around until you return. I am trying to track down demons who may know arms dealers from the time period when the Mormons were massacred. I am convinced that Melchior and Eilers were not the only gunrunners in that era. If nothing else, I'll find out how extensive the outlaw network really is that sells guns down here. I hate that demons cheat."

Mili let that sink in for a moment. She thought that Satan was only after the demons who had supplied the vigilantes with guns. But now it was clear that he was casting a wider net for any and all gun dealers who made deals to provide sinners with guns in Hell. Surprisingly altruistic. Or maybe he was just completely pissed at having his rules broken.

She looked into her husband's blue eyes.

"How many toes do you have on each foot, darling?"

"What did you say?" he muttered surprised.

Mili stepped back and looked at his feet tucked under the table. He was wearing some white crew socks.

"You always hide your toes," Mili said accusingly.

"That's foolish," Lucifer told her and pulled his socks off. He had four handsome toes on each perfectly formed narrow foot.

"How many toes does Little Mardie have?" Mili challenged him.

"Don't know."

"Sriracha?"

"Don't care."

"Jesus?"

"Mili!" the Devil exclaimed. "What's wrong with you?"

Mili glared at her husband, then she turned and walked out of the kitchen. She had never done anything that rude to him before, but her worry over this four-toe thing was eating away at her self-control and familial politeness.

Lucifer got up and followed her. She turned at the front door to find him standing behind her. He put a hand on her shoulder and looked at her.

"Mili?" he asked softly. "What's going on?"

"I'm sorry, love," she replied gently. "It's the deaths. Old and new. And the threats. Real and feared. Plus the sheer awfulness of thinking there is a group of murderers hiding in Hell. Possibly watching *our* every move. All this stuff is getting to me, Lu. Making me act irrationally. I am really sorry."

Satan held her close. Mili leaned against his chest.

"What's with the four-toe fascination?" he asked.

"It's just one more thing," she whispered. "One more thing out of control."

Lucifer didn't understand, but kissed her forehead. Mili opened the door and stepped onto the porch. She turned to say goodbye.

"I'll be back before lunch," she said. "And while I think of it, don't let Jesus watch that cartoon burger show on the telly, please."

"Of course, not," Lucifer replied. "Besides, he'd rather sit in the little red recliner in his bedroom and read."

"Read what?" Mili asked.

"The Gospel of Luke, I think."

"He reads Gospels?" Mili asked surprised.

"He does now. Gabriel dropped that one off for him the last time he visited."

"Did Jesus ask him to bring it?"

"Sort of. Gabriel was telling him a few stories about the Jesus who's up in Heaven."

"Oh, God."

"Don't worry. *Our* Jesus can't read. He just looks at the pictures."

"Well, I guess seeing illustrations of Bethlehem, and the star, and the angels singing can't be all that bad," Mili rationalized. "Has he seen those?"

Lucifer nodded.

"He's up to the crucifixion."

Mili rolled her eyes and drank the last of her coffee. Her baby was looking at *pictures* of Christ's crucifixion. She shook her head and went back to the kitchen to have another cup of coffee.

* * *

Mardie walked in wearing white short shorts that showed off her thirty-six-inch inseam legs, a pink polka-dot tank top, and white leather sandals. Lucifer greeted her while Mili automatically checked out her toes. Five on each pretty foot. Mardie was wearing her blonde hair cut short these days and it flattered her beautiful young face. Mili still wore her hair down to her shoulders. It looked professional, she thought. And Lu liked it that way. Lu and his four-toed feet.

"Am I late?" Mardie asked pouring herself some coffee.

"Pfot just pulled up," Mili answered. "Grab your cup and bring it along."

Mili opened the door and turned to wave at Satan.

"I'll be back before lunch!" she called.

Mardie followed Mili outside and shut the door behind them.

Pfot jumped out of the Volvo and opened up the passenger doors. Mardie thanked him and got in. Mili said hi and got in the side across from Mardie.

"Oh, Mil," Mardie sighed. "You missed *such* a great ending at the Good News Club last night."

Mili shook her head.

"Unless that arse David took a tumble and broke his neck, how good an ending could it have been?"

Mardie grinned.

"Almost as good! He got outed by a prophet named Nathan who told the whole world that David had committed adultery with Bathsheba and arranged the murder of her husband. God also took away their baby. I cried at that part."

"You did?"

"I did. David cried, too."

Mili gazed sympathetically at her sister.

"Well, that kind of puts David in a new light."

"Yes," Mardie agreed. "But without dimming the harsh glare of the truth regarding that bastard Jehovah."

Mili didn't reply. Of course, Mardie was right. Jehovah had let the adulterers live and *killed* the baby. What kind of God was that?

As the Wickett sisters approached Satan's office building they could see Samn demons guarding the entrance, and they passed several more walking up the stairs to Lucifer's office. If anyone were watching Mili and Mardie, they would have quite a challenge getting at them here.

Lucifer had left Moshe's box full of lead slugs sitting on top of his desk. Mili sat in the Devil's chair and Mardie took one at the side of the desk. Mili reached for the box and the lid popped straight off. Mardie jumped back with surprise and watched the lid land on the desk. Pretty cool. Mili was almost sad that the pop-top coffin had never made it into production. She looked inside at the bullets. Then she carefully poured the slugs out onto Satan's asbestos desk.

She counted them. One hundred and forty-six oblong regular lead slugs. Eighteen round ones. She picked up one of the round slugs. It had a deep groove down one side from being shot out of a Colt .36 navy-style pistol. She compared it to the other round balls and quickly determined that every one of them had the same striation. They had all been fired from the same gun.

Mili reached in her purse and pulled out the ball recovered from the murdered demon at the morgue yesterday. Mardie watched as she positioned it next to one of the graveyard slugs. The mark found on all the other round balls was on this one as well.

"Bingo," Mardie exclaimed. "The same shooter who killed a slew of Mormons two hundred years ago *also* shot the Balaam banker yesterday. Son of a bitch."

"He's a son of a bitch no doubt," Mili commented. "Though I suspect he doesn't have that opinion about himself."

"And why would you say that?" Mardie challenged. "He's a murderer and he *knows* it. He hid his crime from your husband for almost two hundred years, but surfaced quick as a hungry shark when he learned that Lucifer had identified the demon who had funded the vigilantes' Colts."

"We think that's all true," Mili agreed. "But the shooter may have also believed that his participation in the Mormon raid was done in the name of justice. Dealing with secret and objectionable activities by Joseph Smith and his Latter-Day Saints."

"You're being needlessly charitable," Mardie complained. "The man is an unconscionable bigot. Killing women and children. He deserves to be here in Hell."

"For sure," Mili agreed. "And I wish that Trump was still around to mete out justice to shitheads who think they can get away with murder down here."

"Well, I'm glad that *Coogan* is not around," Mili said. She looked Mardie in the eyes and spoke deliberately. "His organization is, however, very likely still in business."

"With Lucifer's approval?" Mardie asked.

"I don't know," Mili admitted. "It's not a topic I care to pursue."

Mardie kept silent.

"Let's sort through the rest of the slugs," Mili said. "Each one will have marks from traveling through the various gun barrels. Let's see how we can match them up."

For the better part of an hour the twins compared and grouped the slugs by barrel striations. In the end there were thirteen different groups. Thirteen discrete patterns. Most of the groups were comprised of seven or eight matched slugs. Some had as many as a dozen. All had been shot from army Colt .44s. Except for the group of eighteen balls shot from the navy Colt. The only navy Colt.

Mardie rolled one of the balls around the rough asbestos surface of the desk with her forefinger.

"The navy shooter fired eighteen times," Mardie said. "I wonder how many of those shots connected?"

"We will never know," Mili commented. "Moshe found the slugs scattered in the burial pit. They fell from decaying flesh and bone and wound up at the bottom of the mass grave."

"Thirteen men managed to kill a lot of Mormons."

"That they did," Mili replied. "But we know that several unidentified skeletons are likely raiders killed during the attack."

"I forgot about them," Mardie said. "That actually cheers me up." She paused and stared at Mili. "Hey!" she suddenly cried. "Why aren't there any Winchester rifle slugs in this batch?"

"Easy, Sis," Mili said. "Lucifer only asked Moshe to send over the Colt bullets. The mob killers relied on pistols."

Mili reached into her purse for her mobile phone. She dialed the Devil's mobile number. He answered and his face appeared on her iPhone screen.

"Hi, Mili," he greeted her.

"Thanks for arranging the slugs to be here, darling," Mili said and put him on speaker phone so Mardie could hear. "Looks like thirteen shooters took out all one hundred settlers. Assuming that the eight unidentified male skeletons are shot up vigilantes, that leaves us with five vigilante survivors very probably watching our every move. Also, as you might already guessed, the ball that was removed from the dead banker matched striation marks with slugs that killed Mormons."

"So at least *that* mob survivor is keeping an eye on us."

"Thank you, by the way, for the Samns posted here at your office. I like the idea of them ripping up evildoers."

"The Samns are also armed," Satan told her. "Colts."

"Six-shooters?"

"Damn straight."

"Didn't see those," Mili remarked.

"That's because the Samns don't need holsters," Lucifer told her.

Mili thought about that for a moment.

"Should have worn mine today," Mardie chipped in.

Mili ignored her.

"So, are you two wrapping up then?" the Devil asked.

"Yes. How are the kids?"

"Still sleeping. Except that I get a whiff of smoke from the bathroom once in a while."

Mili glanced apologetically at Mardie. She didn't want Sriracha smoking in her sister's house. It would have to be dealt with. And it looked like it was going to be up to her. Pain in the ass. The kid was as stubborn as she was.

Satan spoke up again.

"I'm coming by the office shortly. Then I'm off to Heaven to request Hellion bodies for Joseph and Hyrum Smith."

"We can arrange to detain you here if you want to postpone that," Mili offered.

"No, no," Satan answered. "But thank you. I have to get it done if we want eyewitnesses to the attack on the Mormons." The Devil smiled a thin smile. "I also want to kick their Mormon asses for hiding from me in the middle of nowhere."

Mili smiled.

Mardie laughed. And snorted.

"By the way," Lucifer continued. "I've been thinking about the small skeletons that Moshe thinks might be children. Doesn't add up. My guess now is that those are the remains of little angels. Pixies and the like. I think they were taken as brides by the Mormon men."

"Oh, my God!" Mardie shrieked.

"I called Moshe on a whim—while I was still smarting from your tirade about my toes, Mili—and asked him to check those skeletons—"

"Don't tell me!" Mili interrupted. "Every one of those small skeletons had feet with only four toes."

Lucifer nodded.

"Pixies, fairies, and sprites. All shot to death."

Mardie ran outside and threw up.

Mili just sat. Holy shit. Only four toes.

CHAPTER ELEVEN

Mili went outside to check on Mardie. She found her sitting on the curb recovering from emptying her stomach on the street.

Mili sat down beside her.

"Poor baby," Mili cooed, putting her arm around Mardie's shoulders. "Are you okay?"

Mardie nodded but didn't say anything.

Mili looked up and watched a person approaching her and Mardie. He was tall, well-built, and dark. If Mili had been aware of American football star Jim Brown, the handsome individual drawing near would have reminded her of that famous athlete. He was dressed in a navy-blue suit, a white shirt, red tie, and black shoes. Mili wasn't sure at first if it was a man or a demon, but something in his walk made her decide that it was a Shapeshifter.

He stopped in the street a few feet from Mili and Mardie. The demon was very upset. His face was distorted by fear and his hands were shaking. Alarmed, Mili stood up.

"Mrs. Morningstar," he said. "You don't know me, but your husband does. My name is Melchior. He and I met recently and he asked me to seek out information concerning demon involvement in providing guns here in Hell. I now have the details he seeks. Is he inside?"

"He is," Mili replied. "Shall I see if he can meet with you?"

"Yes, please," the demon replied urgently. "My life is threatened even as we speak."

"By whom?"

"By the individuals I investigated."

"This is my sister, Mardie. She is feeling ill. I would appreciate it if you'd stay with her for a moment."

Melchior nodded respectfully and went so far as to sit on the curb next to Mardie. Mili hurried up the steps of the Devil's office building and went inside.

Outside, a rotund little green demon with an unhappy face walked down the sidewalk and stopped behind Mardie and Melchior. They turned to see him. He raised a small handgun and pointed it directly at Mardie.

"Where are your guns now, Miss Wickett?" he said in a high-pitched agitated voice.

Mardie stood up and faced the demon.

So did Melchior.

The green demon spoke again.

"You murdered my brother, Eilers," he said angrily. "You shot him a dozen times." The demon shook his head. "I've only got six bullets for you, missy. But I think that will be enough." The demon raised his gun higher. Melchior stepped in front of Mardie and took the demon's first two shots in his abdomen. He did not go down. The demon was furious and fired all of his bullets into the Shapeshifter shielding Mardie.

Even as the green demon fired his final shot, a man running towards him on the sidewalk raised a large handgun and put several shots in the green demon's back. The demon collapsed on the sidewalk. The shooter slowed to a walk and shoved his gun in the back of his belt beneath his suit coat. He was wearing a black suit, a white shirt, a black string tie with a silver bolo embedded with a chunk of turquoise, black boots, and a black Stetson cowboy hat. He was tall and handsome with dark hair, thick eyebrows, and a large, black, bushy moustache that was immaculately trimmed and groomed.

He looked at the Shapeshifter lying dead on the ground. Next to him lay the green demon he had shot. He looked at Mardie and removed his hat.

"Are you hurt, miss?" he asked in a pleasant baritone voice.

In shock at all the carnage Mardie had witnessed she could barely shake her head no.

The man took to his knee and looked at Melchior stretched out on his back. He was still bleeding from the wounds that had taken his life.

"Your husband?" the man asked. "Or a friend?"

"Neither," Mardie croaked. "He had come to see Lucifer and wound up saving my life. The green demon you killed was trying to murder me." Mardie blinked. "Thank you," she said. "You saved my life."

The man gazed the deceased green demon for a moment. He stood back up.

"You are welcome, miss," he told Mardie. "I happened to be in the right place at the right time to render a lady a favor."

Mardie offered her hand.

"Mardie Wickett," she said.

The man extended his hand. It was immaculately clean and his nails were buffed and manicured.

"John Holliday," he said.

"You look and act the part of a perfect gentleman," Mardie said, trying to recover from the double killing she had just witnessed, and feeling amazed that she was not one of the dead.

"Ha!" Holliday said and smiled appreciatively. "You can thank my mother for giving me a proper Southern upbringing," he said pleasantly. "Although I have to credit my profession with my obsession for cleanliness."

"Cleanliness is next to godliness," Mardie said trying to be clever in front of the handsome hunk who had just saved her life.

Holliday chuckled.

"Somehow that didn't work for me," he said affably. "I mean we *are* chatting in Hell."

"Doesn't mean that we can't be clean," Mardie said.

"If not godly," Holliday replied and smiled.

The gallant man took a moment to look at Mardie. He did not miss the fact that her shorts showed off every inch of her shapely bare legs.

"Do you always dress like this?" he had the temerity to ask. "Or did you have some clue that I would in the neighborhood today?"

Both Mardie and John Holliday laughed and turned simultaneously, hearing Mili coming out of the building. She halted on the steps and stared at the fallen bodies. Melchior was dead. Another green demon was dead. Blood had sprayed all over the sidewalk. And a tall man dressed like an undertaker was standing next to her sister. She hadn't been gone five minutes and this catastrophe was what she had returned to.

"John Holliday," the man said as she approached. He bowed his head.

"This is my sister, Mili," Mardie told him. "She is married to Lucifer."

"Pleased to meet you, ma'am," he said. "I have the highest appreciation for the vast improvements made possible down here by your husband's concern for its residents. I must also thank *you* personally for the ice cream stores that have popped up everywhere. They bring back special memories. I had my first taste of vanilla at the Saint Louis World's Fair when I was just a lad."

Mili nodded.

"Some years before you learned to shoot folks with guns, I presume," she said, her voice tense. Her words didn't seem to bother the pleasant man, but *Mardie* objected loudly.

"Mr. Holliday just saved my life, Mili! The green demon claimed he was Eilers's brother, the gunrunner I shot when he tried to kidnap us. Melchior stepped in the way of the bullets and gave his life to save mine. John appeared and shot the green assassin."

Mili looked at Holliday.

"Thank you for protecting my sister from that murderous demon," Mili responded still sounding guarded. "But I would also like to know why it is that you are carrying a weapon in direct violation of my husband's ban on guns in Hell."

"A fair question, dear lady," Holliday replied. "As you surely know, being married to the Lord of Hell, Lucifer grants certain exceptions to his rule to both demons and mortals who may need to protect themselves or extend protection to others. Over the decades that I have been down here, I have been granted the role as a keeper of the peace when troubled times rear their head. My weapon is licensed, and my permission to use it is solely by your husband's authority."

"I apologize for my stiff-necked posture," Mili told Holliday. "I am forever in your debt for saving my sister."

"No, you're not," John replied. "Just doing my part to keep peace in a place that sometimes has trouble maintaining it."

Mili looked down at Melchior. His white shirt was soaked with blood. His eyes were open, steely and confident to the end that he was doing the right thing in saving Mardie Wickett. Mili looked at the green demon. He lay on his face, rivulets of blood still running down his back onto the sidewalk. Staring into the tarmac his eyes were open and horrified that death had found him.

Both Melchior and the green demon suddenly metamorphosed into their ancient angelic bodies. Melchior had been a Power, a tall muscular angel with long blonde hair. His naked body looked like a classic Athenian sculpture of an athlete. Dead, but still in the last throes of his beauty. How sad. There was no rescue for angels who lost their long lives. His musculature and handsome features were preordained to decay and oblivion. The green demon turned into a small, chubby Seraphim. One of the smallest of God's antediluvian host. He was almost pretty with red hair and blue eyes.

"Gone forever," Holliday said memorializing them. "Strange to lose one's immortality by a single moment's choice. One trying to kill you, Miss Wickett," he said looking at Mardie. "And one trying to save you." He paused for a moment, then continued.

"I have to say that I rather fancy the possibility of being brought back again if something happens to my mortal flesh. Couldn't have said that when I first came here. It was hot and unpleasant. There was no way to make money and no way to enjoy life. But now I have a lot to live for in this place. Thanks to the compassion and vision of your husband."

"How long have you been here, Mr. Holliday?" Mili asked growing a little wary of his charms.

"I died in 1887," he answered, "after a long bout with tuberculosis. As a young man I moved from Missouri to Texas and trained as a dentist. I eventually traveled farther west, my longing for adventure piqued when I heard about what a wild and crazy place it was. Knowing that I was doomed to die early, I enjoyed endless nights of gambling, women, and gunfights. It was a time of terrible villains and monumental heroes. Whatever you've read about the American Wild West, it can never capture the outrageous escapade that it all was."

"I don't really know much about that place and time," Mili demurred. "Nothing like it in England's history, you know."

"True," John Holliday said. "It was a lawless time. But righteous men with guns broke the back of the chaos."

"A bit like now," Mardie added. "Even as Hell improves, repeated acts of violence occur more and more. Why should that be?"

"Change upsets those who benefitted from the old paradigm," Holliday theorized. "The rats come out of the woodwork and must be contained."

"You mean killed?" Mili asked.

"In some cases, yes," John replied, sweeping his arm towards the two dead angels. "Sad to say."

An ambulance with its siren blaring drove up and stopped next to the sidewalk where Mili, Mardie, and John Holliday were standing. A crowd of bystanders gathered and stared at the dead bodies. There was shock and fear as they witnessed the bitter end of two of God's ancient angels. Some thought they could not be killed. Others knew they were immortal, but not invulnerable. The two bled-out angels lying on the sidewalk were proof. In the excitement of the moment Holliday walked away.

It wasn't long before Lucifer himself entered the scene. He hugged Mili and Mardie. Then he looked down at the dead angels.

"What happened here?" he asked.

Mili explained the sequence of events and Lucifer reacted furiously that Mardie had been attacked in the open. He recovered quickly, relieved and thankful that Melchior—God rest his lost life—had saved her.

He remembered him as a Power from their days in Heaven together, and had always thought him elegant and handsome. When he became a gunrunner in Hell it had been one more painful realization for Satan that the fallen angels as a whole had turned to lives of lust, greed, and violence. He had also known Eilers's brother, lying here still and emptied of eternal life. His name had been Sorenson, a happy and shy Seraphim who liked to compose songs while lazing in Heaven's meadows with Eilers, watching butterflies and birds. Satan shook his head. "Farewell little fellow. I will not see the likes of you or your brother again."

Lucifer turned to Mili.

"When you're ready, please call Pfotenhauer and he'll run you and Mardie back to her house." He frowned thinking of what he had to do next. "I still have to meet with Jehovah about providing Hellion bodies for Joseph and Hyrum Smith. I'm sure I will get a pain-in-the-ass dressing down from him for not doing it centuries ago. The result of which will be to have Joseph Smith and his brother appear on my doorstep. Shit."

Mili gave Lucifer a kiss on the cheek.

"Be glad it's only two Mormons."

"Two for now. Sooner or later, I will have to request Hellion bodies for the rest of the Mormons who were massacred, be forced to overlook their secret settlement, their clandestine marriages to little angels, and their acquisition of illegal guns. The headstrong actions of the Smith brothers had ripped up things in New York, in Illinois, and then here. I suspect that if they can get away with it, they'll do it again. Goddamnit. This is a no-win situation."

Mili nodded sympathetically. She doubted that the Smith brothers would be getting restored bodies if not for the Devil's desire to obtain the information that *she* needed to locate the vigilantes who had wiped out their Mormon community. Men, women, and some twenty little angels who had somehow become brides of Hell's first Mormons.

Satan looked at Mili and asked her a last question.

"I didn't see the man who shot the little angel and saved Mardie. Who was he?"

"He claimed that you knew him and that as a designated peace-keeper in Hell you gave him permission to carry a gun."

"Well, then, he did his job. Good for him."

"He said that his name was John Holliday."

Satan arched an eyebrow.

"Big guy? Black hair and huge moustache?"

"Yes."

"That's John Holliday alright. He was a famous figure in the old American West. Walked on both sides of the law until he met up with a sheriff he admired and then became both a law-abiding citizen and—when occasions demanded it—a deputy sheriff."

Mili looked confused.

"He said that he was a dentist."

"He was. That's how he got himself the iconic nickname everyone knew him by. Doc Holliday."

"Never heard of him."

Lucifer grinned and shook his head amused.

"Check him out on the internet when you get home. Doc Holliday. And his friend Wyatt Earp."

Lucifer kissed Mili goodbye and walked back into his office building. Doc Holliday and Wyatt Earp, Mili remembered. She could probably kill a few minutes at Mardie's house checking them out. She took one last look at the two bodies. Then she called Pfotenhauer and led Mardie farther down the sidewalk where they could wait in a quiet place. One not covered with dead angels.

CHAPTER TWELVE

Pfotenhauer drove Mili and Mardie back to Mardie's house. She offered to visit with the kids while Mili sat at the kitchen table checking internet files on Doc Holliday and Wyatt Earp. Holliday turned out to be Earp's closet friend, and Wyatt had several brothers. Two of them, Morgan and Virgil, were deputy sheriffs and had worked closely with him in Tombstone, Arizona. Holliday himself had been made a deputy sheriff several times when his quick and accurate shooting hand was needed.

Apparently, the brothers had enemies who didn't like any of the Earps *or* Doc Holliday. Wyatt and his brothers had done a lot to earn that enmity. They were known to jail outlaws on any excuse, and even gun them down if they resisted arrest. A law unto themselves was the common gossip. One particular group of outlaws who called themselves the Cowboys repeatedly threatened to kill all of the Earps and Holliday, too.

Things famously came to a head on October 26, 1881, when the Cowboys were chased through Tombstone by the Earps into a horse enclosure. The OK Corral. Wyatt Earp and his brothers, along with Doc Holliday, shot it out with Cowboys' members Tom and Frank

McLaury and another set of brothers, Ike and Billy Clanton. Some forty Colt .44 rounds were fired. Morgan, Virgil, and Holliday were wounded. Ike Clanton and both of the McLaury brothers were shot dead.

Mili read various accounts of the Earps and this famous gunfight and had to admit that the sheer courage and skills of Wyatt Earp and his deputies made all of them seem like larger-than-life heroes. She called Mardie over.

Mili noticed that Mardie was carrying a paper sack in her hand.

"Sriracha's cigarettes," she told her sister. "Or at least as many packs as I could find."

"Where's Sriracha now?"

"Probably off to get more fags."

"By himself?"

"No. Pfot was still here and Sriracha talked him into taking him to Lucifer's office."

"Where else?" Mili grunted. There was no way to control her son's smoking though she appreciated Mardie's efforts to help. Lucifer's aides would pile Sriracha's arms full with as many cartons of cigarettes as he could carry. She briefed Mardie on the Earps' history with Doc Holliday and the famous shootout at the OK Corral. Then she pulled up images of everyone.

"Oh, my," Mardie uttered. "Check out the 'staches." Every Earp had the same enormous handlebar moustache they'd seen on John "Doc" Holliday that morning. "How much testosterone did those boys have pumping through their bodies?"

"If photographs are any indication," Mili responded, "their wives all have smiles in their pictures."

"Ho!" Mardie blurted out.

"But Doc Holliday didn't have a wife," Mili added.

"What? That man was divine!" Mardie commented. "Gorgeous hair. Perfect clothes. Exquisite manners."

Mili and Mardie looked at each other. Then they spoke at the same time.

"Gay."

"Yet maybe not," Mili advised. "I think that John was such a kind and good man that he chose not to marry so as to avoid leaving a young widow behind. His tuberculosis killed him when he was only thirty-seven."

"So, a true gentleman to the end?" Mardie asked.

"That would be my take."

"Not too many of those around," Mardie moaned.

"Nonsense," Mili objected. "My Lucifer is perfect. So is your Bowles. Not to mention David Ben-Gurion and Moshe Dayan. There are lots of true gentlemen. And they all treat their ladies with love and respect."

Mardie didn't answer.

"You don't agree?" Mili challenged her.

"Sure, I agree," Mardie answered. She looked away for a moment as though sorting through her emotions. She looked back at her sister.

"Maybe sometimes I just think it would be nice to love more than one."

Mili shook her head.

"You've been noodling about the Mormon polygamy too much. Get those thoughts out of your head."

Mardie nodded.

"Still…"

Mili frowned and went back to the internet. She wanted to see if she could track down the kinds of guns the Earps and Doc Holliday had favored in the days of keeping the peace in Tombstone. After a moment she stopped, blinked, then grabbed her mobile and called the morgue at the New Babylon Hospital. She had realized that the dead body of Sorenson, the green demon that had been killed by John

Holliday, had several slugs embedded in his corpse from Doc's gun. She only hoped the angel's cadaver hadn't been already disposed of.

* * *

Mili grimaced. The body was gone. The hospital had standing rules to remove all cadavers for cremation unless a request had been made specifically from Lucifer to hold specific remains for an autopsy. No such phone call had been received so the body of Sorenson—once a sweet Seraphim angel and then a troglodyte-worthy demon—had been released along with the angelic remains of Melchior, a Shapeshifter preceded in that existence as a heavenly Power.

The person Mili talked to did not know who had the contract to dispose of morgue remains, and transferred her to the hospital administration. She got a voicemail recording and hung up. It would be a lot quicker just to ask Doc Holliday himself what kind of gun that he carried. And had used to kill Sorenson.

Mili sat at Mardie's kitchen table. Arms crossed. Feet propped up on the chair next to her. She looked at the kitchen clock. It was back of five. Time for wine. Or ice cream. Her twin sister always kept several pints of Ben and Jerry's Cherry Garcia in the refrigerator freezer. For Mili. She had grown especially fond of it since Jerry Garcia of the Grateful Dead rock group had visited one of her ice cream shops. He'd died on Earth before Ben and Jerry had created the ice cream homage to his fame. But he ate it down here with the unbridled happiness of a little boy.

Mili got up and went to the freezer. She pulled out a carton of Cherry Garcia, popped off the lid, and got a big tablespoon out of the tableware drawer. She grabbed a couple of napkins and sat down to enjoy her treat. Just as she pushed the spoon into the hard ice cream her phone rang.

She picked up the mobile. It was Lucifer.

"Hello, darling," she said as her husband's face filled her phone screen. "Are you back at the office?"

"Just," he said looking miserable.

"How did it go?"

"Jehovah was royally pissed. He asked questions as though he really gave a rat's ass why it took so long for me to locate the Smith brothers. And why I hadn't known they were in Hell. Alive and hiding. Then dead and forgotten."

"Did God grant new Hellion bodies for both of them?"

"He did. Wasn't keen on it as he disapproves of the whole violent history of the early Mormon church. He particularly dislikes the personalities and self-serving actions of Joseph and Hyrum Smith. He made it a point to mention that they went out of their way to stick their polygamous preferences in the noses of their neighbors wherever they settled."

Mili squinted and wrinkled her forehead.

"Why should Jehovah care about that? His good buddy King David had eight wives and a slew of concubines."

"I don't think God actually cares about polygamy. I think he believes that the Mormon proclivity for multiple wives is a divisive maneuver that allows Latter-Day Saints to justify separating themselves and their families from their neighbors and acquaintances."

"For all that he still granted the Smiths new Hellion bodies?" Mili asked.

"Yes," Satan answered. "If for no other reason than to see them in Hell. He was pretty keen on pasting 'eternal' back into their damnations."

"Cold bastard."

"Yes, but thankfully a hands-off bastard, so we'll just keep doing what we want down here and fix up the whole damn place." Lucifer paused and smiled wanly. Just seeing Mili's face on the phone and chatting with her was settling him down after his tense visit with Jehovah.

"I had an unexpected chance to chat with Jesus," he went on. "He said that lots of angels had told him that we had named our youngest after him."

Mili bit her lip.

"And?" she said anxiously.

"He was flattered. Grinned and told me that it was the first non-Hispanic kid he knew who was named Jesus. Ha!"

Satan laughed and so did Mili.

"What a nice fellow he always is," Mili remarked.

"Indeed."

"Especially considering who his father is," Mili said. "I looked up the story on the Earps today," she said redirecting the conversation. "They came across like comic book heroes. Big. Brave. And foes of villains everywhere. Particularly in Tombstone during the Wild West days."

"That's pretty admirable," the Devil agreed. "And did you read about the shootout at the OK Corral?"

"Yes. Almost everyone got shot, but only bad guys died."

"Right. Except the Earps also had their own transgressions. Otherwise, they wouldn't all be down here."

"*They* being?" Mili asked.

"Wyatt, Morgan, and Virgil. They're all in Hell. And you already met John Holliday. As you might expect the Clantons and the McLaurys are down here, too. I have expected an OK Corral repeat for years and years, but it's never happened."

"Are all the Earps allowed to carry guns?"

"Yes. So is Holliday."

"And the Clantons and the McLaurys are not?"

"Never."

"Maybe you have your answer about why there hasn't been another showdown."

"Pshaw."

Mili's eyebrows zipped up.

"Pshaw?" she asked.

"How hard do you think it would be for the Earps' enemies to get weapons down here? Money put in the right hands would buy any top-of-the-line guns."

"Do you happen to know what the Earps' carry?"

"I would think Glocks, Barettas, or Brownings," Satan answered. "They're all semi-automatic weapons of destruction."

"No Colts?" Mili asked almost wistfully.

"There's only one model manufactured any longer. Often recognized as the best six-shooter ever made, it's the Colt .44 Python. But it's such a big, hefty piece that hardly anyone wants to carry one around."

"I wouldn't mind carrying one around," Mili responded enthusiastically. "Could I trade my Derringers for one of those?"

"Based on the recent violent events we've seen, I think that's a brilliant request, love," Lucifer answered. "Let me check on its availability with one or two of the increasingly scarce gun dealers left in Hell. I promise I'll have one for you soon."

"Thanks love. Will you be coming over to Mardie's tonight?"

"Not sure. There's a chance that the Smiths' Hellion bodies may be delivered tonight."

"Call me."

Lucifer blew an air kiss and disappeared from the screen.

* * *

Mili and Mardie cooked macaroni and cheese for the kids and let each child pick out a movie to rent on Netflix. Little Mardie picked *Wonder Woman*. Sriracha chose *African Queen.* (He was trying to learn how to dangle a cigarette in his lips like Humphrey Bogart.) Baby Jesus had to be helped with choices and wound up choosing Disney's *Little Donkey*.

It was the story of a gentle over-the-hill donkey purchased by Joseph to carry his pregnant wife Mary on Christmas Eve.

"Oh no," Little Mardie groaned at Jesus's choice. "Please play my movie first."

"I like *Little Donkey*," Sriracha said. He stared at Little Mardie. "What's wrong with cartoons?"

"Everything!" Mardie answered. "Plus, what would you know? Your brain has been smoked like a ham."

Sriracha didn't have a comeback. Jesus burst into tears sensing he had somehow caused this family squabble. Mili scooped him up and told Little Mardie to bring up her movie first.

"Sriracha, you can watch it, too. But Jesus and I are heading for the kitchen where there are snacks and coloring books."

"Can I smoke?" Sriracha asked.

Mardie shot him a disapproving glance.

"Outside," Mili told him.

"You have more smokes already?" Mardie asked.

"Dad's office crew gave me a few cartons."

Mardie scowled.

"Rotten role models," she hissed.

"You told me that you smoked when *you* were on Earth, Aunt Mardie," Sriracha said in his own defense.

"Not when I was effin ten years old," Mardie snapped.

Mili gave Mardie a withering look.

"And how old *were* you when you started?" she asked her sister.

Mardie answered, but not very loudly.

"Eleven."

Sriracha grinned, then pulled a pack of cigarettes out of his pants pocket.

"Outside!" Mili ordered.

Little Mardie watched her show. Sriracha smoked with two Samn guards on duty. Then Jesus, Mili, Mardie, and Sriracha watched *Little*

Donkey twice. Jesus laughed happily. Mili and Mardie cried. Both times.

Just before nine thirty Lucifer texted Mili. The Smith brothers had been escorted to Hell and David Ben-Gurion had graciously invited them to be guests at the kibbitz while they weighed possible directions for the future. The Devil said he'd be home by ten and attached a photograph of a list of "demands" that Joseph Smith had handed him. Mili flinched. Had he really called them demands?

Mili read Smith's first item. Immediate Hellion replacement bodies for the females who had been killed in the Mormon massacre. They were his wives. Mili shook her head and decided not to read the rest of the list until later. Joseph Smith was going to be a handful. Him and his brother. *And* his eight wives.

That rang some kind of alarm in Mili's head. Who else had eight wives? Henry VIII? No. He had only had six wives. But he was the *eighth* Henry. How did that old English childhood ditty about his wives go? Divorced. Beheaded. Died. Divorced. Beheaded. Survived. Then she remembered that it was the Hebrew King David who had eight wives. And who was an asshole just like Joseph Smith. She later realized that she was wrong. Not about Joseph Smith being an asshole. He *was* an asshole. She was wrong about how many wives he had. His list of demands said that he wanted all of the little pixies replaced. *They were married to him, too.*

CHAPTER THIRTEEN

Mili and Mardie sat in David Ben-Gurion's kibbutz apartment. Moshe Dayan was there. Both Smiths were there as well. The living room was done comfortably with big sofas, overstuffed chairs, and a mahogany coffee table in the center. David kept his books in a separate room that he used for his personal study.

Paula Ben-Gurion was absent, working with friends making charity quilts for distribution to the poor. Lucifer was also absent, claiming work responsibilities. Privately he had told Mili that he couldn't stand being around Thing One and Thing Two, the names he had given Joseph Smith and Hyrum Smith compliments of Dr. Seuss's *Cat in the Hat.*

The Things were sitting together on a big, brown leather sofa. Mili and Mardie were seated in chairs across the coffee table from them. To Mardie's right, Moshe sat in a wooden chair he'd brought in from the kitchen. The Smith brothers looked young. Perhaps in their thirties. They were both black-haired. Joseph was clean-shaven. Hyrum had a goatee. They were taller than average and both were sinewy and lean. They had long, serious faces. Mili noted that neither man seemed to possess any sparkle or animation. She had come to identify those traits with intelligent and creative people. And the lack of those traits with individuals who took themselves too seriously.

There had been very little conversation. The Smiths were still trying to understand what was happening so many years after they and their companions had been murdered. Ben-Gurion had asked Moshe to review the dig findings with them. The Smiths validated Moshe's assumptions and deductions about the massacre of the inhabitants of the Mormon town. Dayan then asked Joseph Smith to describe what had happened. Smith did so, in a somewhat rote manner, as though talking from a prepared script.

"We had no warning that tragedy was about to befall us," he began. "We had deliberately settled far from any other inhabited areas in this place hoping to be left alone. Our experiences in New York and Illinois had taught us that unbelieving neighbors would quickly become jealous of our close fellowship and condemn us for our religious practices."

Joseph paused, then explained.

"By the grace of God, I am the founder and president of the Church of Jesus Christ of Latter-Day Saints. I was personally ordained into this role by Jesus himself who appeared to me. This blessing was subsequently affirmed by three of his disciples; Peter, James, and John.

"Hyrum and I arrived here in 1844 after being martyred by a pagan mob in Illinois.

It was a place that I did not know. Gratefully, I saw that we were not destined to remain alone, being quickly joined by other Mormons. As I mentioned, I did not know the locale in which we found ourselves. I decided that God had located us in a desert place like the freed Hebrew slaves in Canaan. A lonely and vacant place where our faith could grow untrammeled. Sure enough, after less than five years we had seventy-five residents in the town we had built ourselves. For ourselves. We named it Smith Town.

"Imagine our surprise when some inhabitants of this land visited us early on and declared confidently that we were in Hell. Identifying themselves as commercial traders they said they could procure goods for us. While we disowned their mean-spirited judgment of where we had been placed, we were pleased to arrange the transport of our church treasury—several million silver dollars—to be fetched from Illinois. Dealing with those characters was a challenge. But they kept their word and delivered the treasure and proceeded from there to provide further goods and services that we needed."

Mili interrupted Smith with a question.

"At what point did you realize that you really *were* in Hell?"

Joseph Smith arched an eyebrow and looked insulted.

"What are you trying to say, Mrs. Morningstar?" he asked stiffly.

Mili was surprised at the implied denial, but did not let it show on her face.

"Surely the entrepreneurs you dealt with eventually persuaded you that you were indeed in Hell."

"They never brought it up again after trying out that falsehood the first time," Smith replied. "Our church's history is a long and convoluted tale of the lost tribes of Israel fleeing the destruction of the Assyrian army, finding themselves in various inhospitable lands with God unfailingly delivering them to a better place. We knew we were not destined to stay in this harsh land. And whatever this place was, it certainly could not be Hell."

Mili fell silent. She'd deal with Joseph Smith's ignorance—or denial—later on. She nodded and he continued.

"We built houses. Constructed a temple. And erected a school in anticipation of the day when children would bless our population. We planted crops and concentrated on tobacco, a commodity that was treasured by locals who were familiar with the relaxing benefits of the substance.

"Continuing to use the services of intermediaries I was able to meet and marry several interested women from a faraway city that I did not know. They were good folk, though alas, they were not able to bear me children."

"How many of the women in the settlement were your wives?" Mardie clarified.

"All of them," Smith answered without missing a beat. "We lived in harmony and affection."

"What about other men in town?" Mili followed up. "We think there were about sixty or so of them."

Joseph Smith nodded.

"There were fifty-eight males. All good and faithful men. However, they were mostly new converts and were learning the precepts of Mormonism, an essential requirement before being allowed to unite with a woman in marriage."

"So, you were the *only* married man?" Mili asked.

"I was the only man *eligible* for marriage besides Hyrum, who preferred to remain single."

"You had eight wives when the other men had none?"

"Yes," Smith replied without any sign that he was aware of the irony. "God's heroes had many wives. So did I."

Mili, Mardie, and everyone in the room stared at Smith. There was no question that he was totally persuaded of the truth of every word he uttered.

"May I ask when you decided to bring additional females to Smith Town?" Mili asked.

"As I mentioned," Smith responded, "there was no fecundity among the women in my family. No pregnancies, no births, no children." Joseph shook his head, as if to ask how could such a thing happen to a man of such virility? "One of the locals who helped us buy food and farm supplies told me that there were a lot of orphan children—orphan girls—in need of shelter and care. I immediately said that we would take in any girls that were of marriageable age.

"The broker asked what age that would be. I told him that eleven or twelve was the proper age. It was a young enough age to allow formative work with such young women, preparing them spiritually and physically for hard work and bearing children."

Mardie looked at Smith.

"Eleven or twelve years old?"

"Well, some were younger," he allowed. "We may have had some nine- or ten-year-olds."

"How many children did you receive?" Mili asked.

"Ten at first. Ten more later on."

"And these were to be matched up with the single men in town?"

"No, no, no," Smith said tersely. "Whatever gave you that idea? I clearly stated that it was *I* who was in need of progeny. Like Abraham searching for heirs to lead the family of God." Smith looked directly into Mili's eyes. "All of the young women became my wives."

"Over time?" she asked stunned.

"Over the number of nights required to inseminate them."

Joseph crossed his legs and watched Mili, ready for more questions.

Hyrum nodded. See Joseph. Hear Joseph. Speak Joseph.

Mili went on. She turned to the epic event that had wiped out Smith Town.

"What were the circumstances that led up to the raid on your settlement?" she asked.

"There weren't any," Smith answered without emotion. "The attack came out of nowhere. We were attacked by men who rode their horses like the wind. They rushed in so fast and in such numbers, I couldn't tell how many riders attacked us. They were on us without warning and without a reason."

"Who were they?"

"I didn't know then and I don't know now. When we were attacked, we'd been here more than ten years. I never learned who decided that we were all going to die."

"You say that you were surprised when you were set upon," Mili said, "but my husband, Lucifer Morningstar, personally spoke to the arms dealer who filled an order you placed for several dozen rifles."

"That's true," Smith replied. "We ordered them right after we first arrived." Smith's face looked agitated for a moment, then he regained control and continued. "Both Hyrum and I learned in Illinois that we had to have arms to protect ourselves from the wicked wherever we were. Therefore, we immediately bought what we needed to defend ourselves and the people of the town."

"And you received no communication, no ultimatum, no warning from anyone that your Mormon town was being targeted?" Mili asked.

"Not a word. Not a threat. Not so much as a whisper." Smith's face was calm. "Whatever issues the murderers rode in with were never revealed. We managed to shoot several of the villains, but in the end those who remained killed every man, woman, and child."

"Child-bride," Mardie corrected him.

"Child," Smith repeated.

* * *

"What a pair," Mardie declared drinking a glass of Cakebread chardonnay at the

Good News Club. She and Mili were sitting on bar stools waiting for the first reenactment of the night, *Solomon, King of Kings*.

"The talking wanker," Mardie went on. "And the silent wanker. Did Hyrum say anything the whole time?"

"He asked to use a restroom," Mili answered.

"*That* doesn't count," Mardie grumped.

"Well, maybe he doesn't have to say anything," Mili suggested. "He's a vice president.

Ever hear Mike Pence say anything?"

"Who's Mike Pence?"

"Exactly."

"Oh, come on," Mardie answered. "Joseph was stiff and narrow-minded, but I think he told the truth as he understood it."

Mili snorted derisively.

"You mean the part about inseminating the fairies and pixies in rotation?" she asked derisively. I'm sure he did *exactly* that. You're confusing truth with values. He tells the truth. He *doesn't* have any values."

"Well, not your values, anyway," Mardie countered.

"But maybe yours?" Mili shot back. "I remember with some clarity you being rotated through a roster of inseminations during your school years."

Mardie glared at her sister. Then grinned.

"I remember that," she admitted. "Didn't *marry* any of those blokes though."

"You did not."

Mardie held up her wine glass. Bowles filled it and winked. His brown Moroccan eyes were hooded, and his winks spoke volumes about his interest in Mardie and her thirty-six-inch inseam legs. She smiled at him and turned back to Mili.

"So, anyway, why didn't you work Joseph Smith over a little more concerning his marriages to the pint-sized angels?"

"Mardie, the man doesn't believe he's in Hell. Then *or* now. Why would he ever believe that the girls the 'locals' brought him were little angels?"

"So, he really believed that orphaned girls were being rescued and offered a place in his bed? What a creep. Who sleeps with little girls?" she asked disgusted.

"You don't want to know," Mili responded. "British prisons are full of such bounders."

"Until some disgusted prisoner shanks them," Mardie remarked. "And I am beginning to suspect that Joseph Smith's rampant polygamy and his sexual intercourse with 'girls' may have led to Salt Lake City South's destruction."

"Smith Town," Mili corrected her. "But then why were the girls slaughtered and not rescued?"

"Good question," Mardie said. "The killers also murdered the human women in the settlement as well. Heartless bastards."

Mili nodded and worked on her glass of new burgundy. The Good News Club owners had a few cases of France's fresh harvest brought down by Hell's black market entrepreneurs. Hmm. It was a bit sour. Actually, almost as sour as she felt. She had not enjoyed the interview with Joseph. He lacked vitality. He lacked a human touch. He acted more like a Mormon icon than a caring leader. Plus, the whole point of talking to him was to find out who had ambushed the town and killed everyone. And that had not happened.

David Ben-Gurion met with Smith after he had finished his time with Mili, and demonstrated great kindness to him and Hyrum. He did give Mili a knowing smile and a wink when Joseph had talked at length about the wandering lost tribes of Jews settling back when in upstate New York. Right. If Smith had claimed that they became Orthodox diamond dealers off Times Square Ben-Gurion might have taken him more seriously.

He told Mili when she and Mardie were leaving that he'd offered to provide temporary accommodations on the kibbutz for the Mormon leaders while they made plans for their future. They had been polite and appreciative, but Ben-Gurion had developed instant anxieties when Joseph had asked to be put in touch with "locals" who could fetch things he needed from Earth.

"Like what?" Mili had asked him.

"He didn't say," David whispered.

Mili had spoken with Lucifer before she and Mardie had returned to town to attend the reenactment. She told him that she hadn't gotten any productive information from Joseph and Hyrum Smith.

"Pair of pricks," was his take.

"Mardie's view precisely," Mili replied.

"And *your* view?" the Devil asked.

"Not sure," Mili said slowly. "Joseph Smith seemed almost hollow. Devoid of human warmth. Just a symbol. As if he were not a flesh-and-blood person. It felt spooky."

"I don't like him," Satan said. "But I try and keep in mind that he's had a rough go of it. Almost from the first moment he claimed that the angel Moroni revealed the golden tablets to him."

"Good time for me to ask you whether there even *is* an angel Moroni?"

"No, there's not. But Smith might be mispronouncing his actual name. Many of the first angels had Semitic names echoing the fact the Elohim spoke a language that eventually evolved into Aramaic."

Mili thought about that for a minute. She was not in a mood to unscramble arcane angel names. In fact, she was not in much of a mood to do *any* kind of work after her long, unproductive session with Joseph Smith. Oh yeah. And Vice President Hyrum. She told Mardie on the drive back to New Babylon that she was looking forward to the reenactment that night. Last night's performance had been about David. His tale would continue this evening with the story of his son and heir, King Solomon.

"Wasn't he the chap who married a thousand wives?" Mardie asked.

"Yes, he was," Mili responded. "Should have been the world's first Mormon."

"Maybe he was," Mardie said and grinned. "You know, the missing tribes thing?"

Mili laughed out loud.

Best she'd felt all day.

CHAPTER FOURTEEN

Mili drank her new harvest burgundy. The red had a bit of a snap, but finished smooth. Sort of what Mili had thought sex would be when she first imagined it at age eleven. Took her a few relationships to realize that *that* experience only applied to the orgasms she arranged on her own. With men, coitus was more like who's knocking at my door only to find that when she opened the door they were gone.

"I like it here," Mili told Mardie. "I mean the club."

"So, do I," her sister agreed.

"Why is it that we don't come here more often?"

"Lots of reasons," Mardie answered. "Staying at the kibbutz. Keeping an eye on the kids. Drilling down on detective cases. Still, there's no reason why we can't try to see more performances."

"Coming here the last two nights is a good start," Mili told her.

Mardie nodded happily and raised her glass. Mili touched it with hers and the twins drank to each other and their time together.

Bowles smiled at the pair and offered to escort them to a table near the stage. Mardie noticed that there were five chairs at the table.

"Will us sharing this table bother the folks who reserved it?" Mili asked.

Bowles shook his head.

"I am absolutely positive that the three people coming will be delighted to have your company."

Mili gazed at Bowles with a quizzical expression on her face.

He explained.

"Dr. Albert Einstein reserved this table. He is bringing Dr. Hugh Everett and

Dr. Stephen Hawking."

Mili was stunned.

"Hawking is in Hell?" she asked.

"Only for a visit," Bowles told her. "Your husband got permission on his last trip in Heaven for Dr. Hawking to come down to meet Dr. Einstein on his birthday. He's here now and Professor Einstein decided to have some fun with his young admirer and bring him to the club."

"Wow," Mili murmured. "Stephen Hawking."

"And the one and only Hugh Everett," Mardie added happily.

"So, may I seat you ladies?" Bowles asked.

"Only after they arrive," Mili stipulated.

Bowles nodded and moved down the bar to serve some new folks.

"I think I'm too dumb to sit at their table," Mardie stated glumly.

"Nonsense," Mili corrected her. "Plus, all you have to do is look beautiful. Hawking has never met you. Everett has always had a crush on you. And Einstein was once a player. Remember?"

"Are you talking about his trip to Tel Aviv?"

Mili nodded.

"He went muff diving when his wife was waiting on the boat." Mardie giggled. "The point is," Mili went on, "all three of those brainy men love women. Particularly knockouts like you. Good thing you didn't wear something showing off your cleavage or they'd have no idea what the performance is about."

"Flatterer."

"Trust me," Mili told her. "Big brains are no defense against big boobs."

Bowles refilled both women's glasses and nodded toward the front of the café. The scientists had arrived. White-haired Einstein wore brown wool pants, a green wool sweater, and a corduroy sports jacket. Everett had on a Boston Red Sox baseball cap, overalls, and a white T-shirt. Stephen Hawking, young and fresh-faced, confident and handsome, walked in arm-and-arm with Eddie Redmayne. Both were tailored in immaculate suits, white shirts, and ties.

Bowles intercepted everyone and ushered them to the bar. Mili and Mardie stood up and were quickly embraced by both Einstein and Everett, receiving hugs, laughter, and smooches on the cheek. Albert Einstein introduced Stephen Hawking and told the sisters that Hawking had the distinction of once having answered an interviewer's question by saying that if he had to choose between meeting Albert Einstein or Marilyn Monroe, he'd pick Monroe. Hawking flushed. Everyone else roared. But Einstein—the most famous of all twentieth-century scientists—did not offer a retraction.

Einstein introduced Mili and Mardie to Hawking and Redmayne while Bowles took drink orders from the men. He then escorted everyone to their reserved table. He brought an extra chair and in moments returned with a Crown Royal Perfect Manhattan for Hugh Everett. a flute of Cristal champagne for Stephen Hawking, a vodka and tonic with lime for Eddie Redmayne, and a snifter of cognac for Albert Einstein.

"How's Heaven?" Mili asked Hawking.

"I have to say that the company is extraordinary," Hawking replied. "Not as gorgeous as the present company, mind you, but lunch with Isaac Newton? And then dinner that same night with Galileo? How can you beat that?"

"*The* Galileo?" Mili asked.

"Yes," Hawking answered. "He recanted his views on the solar system and was reembraced by the Catholic church. Saved *his* ass."

"And what saved yours?" Everett asked lighting up a smoke.

"I asked Gabriel right off the bat about that," Hawking answered and shook his head.

"He told me that my humility had redeemed me."

"Whoa," Eddie Redmayne commented.

"Yes," Hawking said. "He said my voice appearances on *Futurama* and *The Simpsons* television shows had given pleasure to folks all over the world."

"Nice," Einstein said, pleased to see a healed and happy Stephen Hawking sitting across from him. "Didn't have voiceover cartoons in my day," he mentioned. "If they had, I might be up there keeping you, Newton, and Galileo company."

"And Leonardo Da Vinci," Hawking added.

"Da Vinci is in Heaven?" Einstein cried. "The inventor of the most savage siege machines of the Renaissance?"

"Yes," Hawking said. "His religious paintings saved *his* ass."

"And how are you, Hugh?" Mardie asked.

"Everything is very good," Everett responded. "Thanks for asking. I'm residing in an alternate world as you know, so some things are different—not necessarily in a bad way—but sometimes challenging. In my world Donald Trump is a progressive president serving his third term."

Redmayne choked on his drink. Mili patted his back. Hawking downed his champagne and stared at his empty glass.

Hugh Everett kept *his* eyes on Mardie.

"You look like you've been through some alternate stuff as well," he said admiringly. "You've always been gorgeous, however."

"Thanks for noticing, Hugh," Mardie answered. "Remember when Mili and I asked you and Dr. Einstein about using time bridges to go back to England and track down Jack the Ripper?" Hugh nodded. "We found him and shot him dead. Then he found me in Hell afterwards and returned the favor."

Hugh's face looked stricken.

"He killed you?"

"Yes. But in the end, he was made to disappear for good while I was brought back with a younger body."

"A younger *state-of-the-art* body," Hugh clarified. "I trust that the essential Mardie was not affected, however?"

"Not at all," Mardie answered. "I just get laid more often."

An embarrassed silence fell over the table. Bowles noticed and brought another round of drinks. As he did, the overture began playing on the club speaker system signifying that the reenactment was starting. Conversation at the table resumed nonetheless, moving onto the latest and greatest question in quantum physicist circles. For the first time ever a new theory proposing the existence of a pre-Universe *before* the Big Bang had been offered by a quantum physicist named Maha Salah. It was entitled "Non-singular and Cyclic Universe from the modified GUP."

The scientists chatted through the opening of the reenactment while Mili and Mardie watched, enjoying the wise but libidinous King Solomon trying to remember the names of his wives. Einstein, Everett, and Hawking kept on discussing the controversial quantum physics paper non-stop. Eddie Redmayne opted to enjoy a string of vodka and tonics with lime through the whole reenactment. Mardie noticed that Redmayne not only ignored the quantum physics discussion, but he didn't pay much attention to the play either. But she forgave him. After all, not everyone had an interest in quantum physics. Or acting.

* * *

After the play ended most of the Good News Club patrons headed home, including the scientists. They were adjourning to Dr. Einstein's house to talk into the night. Mili and Mardie did hugs, kisses, and farewells and adjourned to the bar to drink into the night.

"I am starting to feel like a lush," Mili said choosing a glass of port for her nightcap.

"So what?" Mardie responded. "A hangover is the worst thing you can expect down here."

"I wonder about impaired brain functions," Mili went on. "You know. Reduced ability to solve issues."

"Just being able to worry about it probably means you're fine," Mardie told her.

Mili sipped her port and thought through the weird components of her current case. Mormons founding a secret settlement in Hell. Joseph Smith marrying eight women down here and "marrying" another twenty pixies. Then an arms race between the settlers and enemies they didn't even know about, resulting in the massacre of the entire population.

Mardie nudged Mili. She spoke with breathy enthusiasm.

"Look!" she gushed. "Is that Sean Connery coming in the front door?"

Mili glanced at the club entrance. A tall man stood there dressed in a black suit, a white shirt, a black string tie with silver tips and a silver bolo, and black boots. He held a black Stetson cowboy hat in his hand. And he *did* look like Sean Connery. His face was incredibly handsome. His posture was erect. His thinning hair was white and groomed perfectly. He had a huge, white, walrus moustache and intelligent bright blue eyes. Who was this man? And what was he doing here so late?

"Stand up," Mili told Mardie. "Do you have a gun in your purse?"

"One of my Colt revolvers."

"Unsnap your purse in case you have to grab it."

Mardie frowned.

"You're worried about an old cowboy?" she complained.

"Cowboy or Shapeshifter?" Mili asked in a hushed voice. "Open your purse."

Mardie did. Both women watched as the man glanced at the empty tables on the club floor and then saw them at the bar. He walked over and looked at Mardie and then at Mili. His blue eyes were intense, but at the same time amused.

He spoke to Mili in a clear tenor voice, very firm, very confident, and very youthful for his age.

"Do I have the pleasure of addressing Mrs. Milicent Morningstar?"

Mili nodded formally.

"I am Mili," she said.

"Pardon my intrusion," the man replied politely. "I have been in communication with Lord Lucifer and he encouraged me to speak to you in person. He kindly advised me of your presence here."

"Then you must have a very pressing issue," Mili replied.

"I bear very important information about the massacre at Smith Town."

"How would you know the name of that town?" Mili asked sounding like an official interrogator. "It's been lost almost two hundred years."

The man smiled a thin smile.

"I have acquaintances who knew the secret town. Visited it. And saw that it was run like a cult. You met one of the folks who saw it. John Holliday."

"Yes, we met Mr. Holliday," Mili acknowledged. "Who are you?"

"My name is Wyatt Earp."

Both Mili and Mardie stared at the most famous sheriff who had ever put their lives on the line to tame the American Wild West. Holliday had died young. Almost at the same time Joseph Smith and his brother had been killed in the Illinois jail. But Earp had lived past the age of eighty and came to Hell looking like the retired successful lawman that he was.

"I've heard of you, Mr. Earp," Mardie said cheerfully. "You had quite a life."

Earp smiled at her kind words.

"I did, indeed. The kind of life that lands you in damnation, dear lady. But I wouldn't change a thing. I never once engaged in the use of guns without judging my actions to be fair and justified. And I died peacefully in my bed. I am not embarrassed or regretful of any deed credited to me."

"Eloquently stated, Mr. Earp," Mili answered. "How can I be of help?"

"I propose that you, Lord Morningstar, and your sister Miss Wickett," he nodded towards Mardie, "come to my house tomorrow night for dinner and a discussion of the history of Smith Town. Diners will include my brothers Virgil and Morgan. They have first-hand knowledge of the rise and fall of the secret Mormon settlement."

"I will have to check my husband's availability," Mili answered.

"I understand," Earp replied. "But may I say that you and Miss Mardell are unconditionally invited to attend even if your husband cannot."

"Then you may count on me—" Mili said and turned to Mardie who nodded instantly, "—and my sister, Mardie."

Wyatt bowed his head.

"I am honored. I live on my ranch, the Earp Ranch, which can be easily located using the internet."

"Do you have a mobile phone, Mr. Earp?"

"I do not. However, our website lists a home phone number if you need to be in touch." Earp paused, then went on very politely. "Do either of you ladies have dietary restrictions I should be aware of? I raise beef for a living and am planning on grilling up barbeque steaks tomorrow night with all the fixins."

"Fixins?" Mardie couldn't help but ask.

Earp smiled nicely.

"Whiskey, bourbon, vodka, and gin," he answered and winked.

"Put me down for whiskey," Mardie said.

"Grilled steaks would be wonderful," Mili answered. "Thank you for your graciousness."

Wyatt Earp bowed deeply from the waist. Then he turned and left the club. Mili and Mardie watched him go. Bowles returned and asked if they wanted refills.

"Yes," Mili told him. "Port and—" she looked at Mardie.

"—Whiskey," her sister said.

Both Bowles and Mili looked surprised.

"Might as well practice," Mardie explained and grinned.

"Port and whiskey," Mili told Bowles. "And leave the bottles."

CHAPTER FIFTEEN

Mili got an early call the next morning from Moshe Dayan at the kibbutz. He wanted her to know that the newly-arrived Smith brothers had gotten very busy.

"They've met with a succession of black market vendors," Moshe told her. "Demons. I recognized some of them. One was a Shapeshifter who specializes in retrieving money or personal possessions left behind on Earth. He likes to dress up like one of the chaps on the television show *Pawn Stars*.

"Another was a Balaam who works in the banking industry importing surplus military tents and associated camping supplies. My guess is that the Smith brothers are planning on heading out to some other part of Hell to set up shop again. I have no idea where that might be, but I'll guarantee you that wherever they settle, your husband's demon network will be keeping a sharp eye on their activities this time around.

"Another supplier—yet another small green demon—was a gun dealer. I fear that he may be a relative of the two greens you've encountered, Eilers and Sorenson."

"How *big* is that family?" Mili asked.

"Extensive. They appear to get along quite well and most of them ply the family trade. Weapon procurement."

"Any of it legal?"

"The stuff they do on Earth, Satan doesn't care about," Moshe answered. "But they are rumored to carry on significant illegal trade in Hell, too."

"So, you think the Smiths are preparing to arm themselves before attempting to found another settlement down here?" Mili asked.

Moshe nodded.

"They clearly don't trust anybody," he told Mili. "And why should they? The last time they homesteaded down here they had the shit shot out of them."

"Graphic," Mili said. "I wonder if they have given any more thought as to where they really are. How can they continue to ignore that this is Hell when they are literally back from the dead?"

"Who knows?" Moshe said and shook his head. "But it's obviously impossible for them to be down here according to any of their religious tenets. Which actually is not all that unusual. We all filter out whatever we choose not to believe. Mormons believe that they are the descendants of the Chosen People led by Jehovah to the new Promised Land. I don't think there were any stops in Hell on that itinerary."

"Do I need to visit the Smiths again?" Mili asked.

"Can't see why," Moshe answered. "Although if you'd bring Mardie along in her short shorts and Colt holsters, I'll keep her company while you visit them."

"Ha!" Mili snorted. "What about *me* in short shorts?" she teased.

"You're forgetting that I know about your husband's secret torture operations," Moshe replied softly. "*You* in short shorts? As divine as that would be, it would likely cost me my only remaining eye. No thanks!"

"Good for you Moshe," Mili said laughing. "You chose wisely. Thanks for the updates on the Smiths. Please call me when they head out." Mili paused briefly. "You will have folks tracking them no doubt?"

"Absolutely. And, by the way, there was another demon who met with Joseph—alone—whom I did not recognize. He was the handsomest demon I've ever seen. Long black hair done in dreadlocks. A pale face. And dressed in an odd ensemble. He was wearing a purple suit and a large white hat with a big plume."

Mili frowned.

"How long did they talk?" she asked.

"Ten minutes or so. The demon made a lot of notes on a pad."

"All right," Mili responded. "That character is a mystery to me. Pleases keep me posted."

"Of course," Moshe said.

"Goodbye. Be careful, Moshe."

"Thank you, Mili. If something happens, make sure my Hellion comes back with my eyepatch."

"I promise," Mili replied and pressed the *Off* button on her phone.

So, the Mormons were moving rapidly to get out of the kibbutz and stake out a place of their own again. Despite the complete disaster that Joseph Smith had brought down upon himself and his followers ages ago, he was apparently bent on repeating it. Secret settlement. Abundant cash for building materials, supplies, and guns. Isolation from anyone else in Hell.

And who was the strangely dressed demon taking notes? Why was Smith meeting with him? "Oh, my God!" Mili gasped. The answer was staring her in the face. Joseph was already arranging for new pixies to be delivered.

She called Pfotenhauer instantly.

His worn but friendly octogenarian face filled her little phone screen.

"Mrs. Mili," he proclaimed happily. "How are you?"

"Busy, busy, thanks Pfot. How are you?"

"I'm well, thank you for asking. Will you be needing a ride, ma'am?"

"Not now, thanks. I'm spending some catch-up time with the children at Mardie's house, and winding my way slowly through the thicket of seemingly unconnected data that I've gathered on my current investigation."

"Oh, but isn't connecting the dots part of the challenge of such cases?" Pfot asked enthusiastically. "And I have to believe that only the very toughest investigations made it onto your desk at Scotland Yard."

"That's very kind, Pfot. But these kinds of cases are also very frustrating. In this particular situation I am beginning to believe that an awful piece of history is about to repeat itself and I am trying to do everything in my power to prevent it."

Pfot's face turned very serious.

"Do you need any guns, Mrs. Mili?"

"No. Mardie and I are adequately armed. You were there when she used her six-shooters defending us at the Mormon dig."

"Aye. Saw the demon body with my own eyes. Turned into a wee angel it did."

"Pfot, I called to pick your brain about a demon who Moshe saw carrying on a private conversation with Joseph Smith. He was wearing a purple suit and a somewhat flamboyant hat with a large feather. Do you know who that individual might be?"

Pfotenhauer's face looked troubled.

"I know a demon fitting that description," Pfot answered. "He's a Shapeshifter whose name is Osmodeus. Goes by Oz. He claims that he is the bastard offspring of King David's liaison with a succubus. He is designated in the Kabbalah as the demon of lust."

"So, he's not an angel?"

"Farthest thing from it," Pfot said vehemently. "He is true demon, cursed by God, and deserving only annihilation."

"I've never run into a true demon before," Mili said. "I guess I thought all the demons were fallen angels."

"No," Pfot said. "Jesus had intense and frequent warfare with powerful demons when he lived on Earth. In particular he warred against Persian and Canaanite jinn."

Mili shook her head. She knew nothing about such creatures.

"What does Osmodeus peddle?"

"He comes down to Hell from Earth where he dwells. His specialty is providing pixies willing to have sex with Hellions."

"Is there any chance he might have supplied Joseph Smith with such creatures when he inhabited the secret Mormon settlement?"

"A very good chance," Pfot replied. "Oz has a virtual monopoly on the trade as no fallen angels will pimp in that manner."

"Does he coerce the pixies? Trick them? Lie to them? Force them down here against their will?"

"No. He's a straightforward businessman who usually buys his females from those who claim to be in possession of them."

"They're slaves?" Mili gasped.

"Yes. Owned and exploited until they are sold, dumped, or die. Master Lucifer knows about these captive females, mostly bound to Hellions and demons."

"Christ, Pfotenhauer," Mili swore. "I'm appalled. Sex slaves? How long has this been going on?"

"I don't know, ma'am," Pfot answered, clearly embarrassed. "I would guess since the beginning."

Mili shook her head. Lucifer had never mentioned this sex trade. Joseph Smith had apparently acquired pixies from Osmodeus before. And he was going to do it again.

She spoke to Pfotenhauer again.

"Does Osmodeus also deal in human girls or women?"

"Not women. Too much risk that someone would report him. And girls *never*."

"Pfot, find out how I can meet with Osmodeus."

"That's a tall order, Mrs. Mili," Pfot answered shaking his head. "Given who he is and given who you are, he will never agree."

"Would he meet with Mardie?"

"About acquiring *a slave girl?*"

"Well, why not?" Mili replied trying not to smile at Pfot's dumbfounded expression.

"How about a meeting with Moshe Dayan?" Pfot counter-proposed.

"Okay," Mili agreed. "Please try and arrange a meeting between Osmodeus and Moshe. Tell the demon that Dayan wants a pixie. Don't explain. Just tell him that price is no object."

"As you wish, Mrs. Mili," Pfot responded dutifully. "I'll find out from the demon network how to contact him as quickly as possible."

"Thank you, dear Pfot. Call me anytime. Ta, dear boy."

"Indeed," Pfot said. "Ta, ta."

* * *

It was seven o' clock and Mardie and Mili were sitting at a table near the front of the stage at the Good News Club. They had come to the club for their third night in a row. It was the last play in the special reenactment trilogy, *David and Bathsheba*, *Solomon, King of Kings*, and *Candace of Ethiopia*.

"I can't believe that we're here again!" Mardie exclaimed happily. "Drinking our asses off."

"Would you rather be at Avalon Lanes watching Hell's worst villains knocking the same pins down over and over?"

"Maybe we could bribe the pixies working *there* to rig the pin machine so that *no* pins could be knocked down?"

Mili looked at Mardie.

"You're not forgetting that they got caught taking bribes from King Edward when they set him up for his so-called perfect game?"

Mardie nodded.

"I remember," she answered. "Those wenches were lucky Lucifer didn't fire them on the spot."

"He did turn the tables on them, however," Mili said. "He made the pixies reset the software every time the British team bowled, giving *every* player a perfect game. Besides, you don't fire pixies. They're slaves. They have nowhere to go."

Mardie stared at her sister.

"Those cheaters were slaves?" she repeated, trying to digest that surprise information.

"Yes. There are no *Hellion* slaves down here, but in ages past, pixies were enslaved by demons and sold to men to provide services like housekeeping, cooking, nannying, and such."

Mardie was incredulous.

"Milicent Wickett! You've known about that and yet you couldn't tell me how Joseph Smith managed to provide himself with *child* brides. He bloody bought them!"

Mili told Mardie she had just found out from Pfotenhauer about the secret pixie trafficking down here provided by the demon Osmodeus. Mardie had heard of Osmodeus—the vile demon of lust—and knew that he claimed to be spawned by a fallen angel that had seduced King David. She did not know that the evil creature sold pixie slaves.

"That is *so* nasty," Mardie said and shook her hands as though to fling off such filth.

"David still managed to be a man after God's own heart," Mili reminded her.

Mardie scowled.

"Every time I hear that, the more glad I am to be down here with decent people."

"Mostly decent," Mili corrected.

"Yes. Mostly decent."

"And made even more pleasant because David is *not* down here. He's in Heaven with Bathsheba and who knows how many of his slew of wives."

"Did you know that Absalom, David's son, is down here?"

"No. But I think he should be," Mardie said. "Isn't he the one who rose up in rebellion against David?"

"Can you blame him?"

"Not really. But a lot of innocent people get killed in civil wars."

"Fact is, that's not why he's in Hell. Absalom's half-brother, the Crown Prince Amnon, raped Absalom's sister Tamar. David refused to punish him so Absalom killed him and fled the kingdom. David let him return after three years, but he refused to speak to him even though Absalom was now David's oldest surviving son and heir to the throne. Absalom finally blew up and seized the throne. His father fled, but rallied his army to eventually defeat Absalom's rebel troops and slay his rebellious son."

"Terrible story," Mardie said.

"Amnon's murder is Absalom's sentence of damnation."

"Sheesh lareesh," Mardie mumbled. "Is Amnon down here, too?"

"No. He's in Heaven. Rape is not a damnable crime."

"Fuck!" Mardie almost screeched.

Folks around the bar jumped at her outburst.

Mardie held up her hand as if to stop her twin from telling her anything more.

Mili nodded.

"Tonight's play is about Solomon, not David. Love, adventure, and falling in love with a brave and brilliant African queen." She looked encouragingly at Mardie. "What's not to like?"

"All right," Mardie said begrudgingly. "I hope so. But no surprises. This has already been a night of way too much information."

"And not nearly enough wine," Mili said and waved for Bowles to come over.

CHAPTER SIXTEEN

Mili sat at Mardie's kitchen table nursing a headache. She didn't know exactly what time it was, but bright sunshine pouring through Mardie's windows was making her squint. She put a hand above her eyes and looked at the clock on the wall. Back nine already. She had to get moving. She finished her second cup of coffee and went off to get showered and dressed.

Pfotenhauer was picking her and Mardie up at ten o'clock to return to the kibbutz. The slave dealer Osmodeus had agreed to an appointment with Moshe Dayan. Mili wanted to be there for Moshe. There was no reason to believe that the demon could be trusted in any way. She had already removed the Derringer from her purse and replaced it with the new Colt .44 Python Lucifer's aides had fetched for her.

It had a blue steel barrel and a brown wooden handle. The Devil told her to hold the gun with both hands. Point it at her target. And pull the trigger. As often as she wanted. And the closer she was to the target the better.

"Why do you keep saying target?" she asked him. "If I have to use this gun, I will be pointing it at a person or a demon."

Satan shrugged.

"A person or a demon only takes on its endangered status *when you deem it a target.*"

That didn't make sense to Mili, but she thanked Lucifer for the weapon. She liked the gun's heft and imagined its power. She remembered Mardie shooting the green demon with her Colts. Her sister's weapon had been overwhelming. But it was old. How much more force would the new Python be able to muster?

Mili towel-dried her hair and combed it out. She put on a white cotton skirt that dropped to her knees and a tie-dyed tank top. She slipped on white sandals, grabbed her big brown leather purse, and headed out the door at ten o'clock. Mardie was waiting outside already. Samns were on duty. They nodded at Mili.

Pfot greeted Mili and opened a passenger door for her. Mardie got in the other side and reclined her head against the headrest. She put a forearm over her eyes.

"Don't talk," Mardie said without looking at Mili.

Mili noticed that her sister had brought a big red-and-black plaid tote bag instead of a purse.

"Got your Colts in there?" Mili asked.

"Yes. Don't talk."

She didn't.

* * *

At the kibbutz Mardie opted to stay in the car. Her hangover was so severe that she felt she wouldn't be of any help when Moshe met with the lust demon. Mili agreed with her and asked Pfot to fetch Mardie a glass of cold water and keep an eye on her.

Moshe appeared and approached the car. He had on black slacks and a short sleeve white shirt. Mili noticed that his shirt was wrinkled. Had he slept in it overnight? Ha. Israeli men didn't need to be circumcised for one to identify their ethnicity. One only needed to look for black slacks and short sleeve white shirts.

"Dear Mili," he said and gave her a nice hug. Most men remained stiff as boards when they embraced a female friend, but Moshe gave a nice hug without any hint of sexual impropriety. Pretty good achievement for a famous lady's man. He stepped back and gazed at her face.

"Oh," he said. "You are under the weather."

Mili shook her head.

"Just recovering from being under the influence."

Moshe smiled a kind understanding smile.

"Mardie, too?" he asked.

"Yes. She's staying in the car."

Moshe looked dismayed.

"She'll be fine," Mili told him. "I'm just sorry that her Colt revolvers won't be handy when we meet Osmodeus."

Moshe brushed off her concern.

"The demon has nothing to gain by threatening us. Pfot's demon connections assured him that Osmodeus is an established dealer who has plied his wares successfully since the days of the great kings of Jerusalem."

"They weren't so great," Mili disagreed. "Mardie and I drank God knows how much wine sitting through three reenactments about David and his descendants. Totally pathetic. I can't believe the Jews put up with that guy."

"Are you serious, Mili?" Moshe responded. "Compared to putting up with Jehovah, David was a piece of cake."

Mili stared at Moshe and then laughed out loud.

"Yeah, good point," she conceded. "But David was still a wanker."

Moshe nodded.

"Yep, a man after God's own wanker."

Mili laughed again, surprised at Dayan's irreverent humor.

"We'll wait here for Osmodeus to arrive," Moshe said. "He asked if it would be okay to meet in his car."

"*In* his car? That's weird."

"Maybe. But lots of deals get made in cars," Dayan noted.

So do lots of babies."

"Not in Israel. *That* happens in the co-ed army barracks during military service."

"I didn't know that."

Mili turned her head to watch a long, cream-colored Mercedes-Maybach 57 coupe drive up and park in front of the kibbutz administration buildings. She had seen a few of those in London. They were always owned by the mob.

"Bastard has some money," she said.

"Pfot said he leases it," Moshe responded.

"It's still an immodest statement about how much money he makes *selling pixies*."

Moshe nodded.

He and Mili walked over to the luxury car. The chauffeur, a small thin black man, stepped out and opened a back door. He invited Moshe to get in. Mili followed him into the backseat. A razor-thin man with black dreadlocks and a handsome face looked back at them from the front passenger seat with a distinctly unhappy expression. He was wearing a purple Zoot suit from the 1930s. He looked like a pimp cast for a Hollywood movie. Was he serious? Or playing it for camp?

Osmodeus didn't introduce himself and spoke directly to Moshe.

"Did Pfotenhauer tell you the cost of a pixie?"

"Yes," Moshe replied. "Price is not an issue."

"Is there another?" Osmodeus asked with a suspicious tone in his voice.

"Only if you want to talk about selling those little creatures to Joseph Smith."

"Fuck off."

Moshe smiled.

Mili frowned.

Moshe persisted.

"The last batch you sold him were murdered when his Mormon town was attacked."

Osmodeus' expression didn't change.

"Not my business. Not your business."

Moshe arched an eye.

"You're kind of a touchy bastard," he told the demon.

"Don't waste my time. Are you buying or not?"

"How about if I give you the price of a pixie just for information about your new transaction with Smith?"

"$250K. Let me see the cash."

Moshe opened the small black leather valise he had brought along and lifted out several rolls of gold coins.

"Two hundred gold American twenty-dollar eagles," he told Osmodeus. "Spot price for gold this morning was $1,924 an ounce. You're actually getting a significant bonus. Help you pay for your wheels."

"Put the gold back in the case. Hand it forward." Moshe didn't move. "Please," the demon added. Moshe put the coin rolls back and handed the valise to the demon.

"How many pixies did Smith order?" Moshe asked.

"Ten."

"For him and Hyrum?"

"Just for himself."

"Will they take long to deliver?"

"Three days."

"Here?"

"No. At a temporary camp he is establishing. Away from kibbutz property."

"Did he get his pixies from you before?"

"I thought that was obvious," Osmodeus said.

"Then you must have information about who raided Smith Town two hundred years ago," Mili told him.

Osmodeus scowled.

"I have heard that ancient issue raised twice in the last few days. It is not in my interest to deal with it."

"Does that mean you know who did it?"

"That means I am not going to talk about it."

Mili met Osmodeus' threatening glare.

"Have you never lost anyone you cared about?" she asked.

"I care about myself, madam. What you are talking about happened centuries ago. If you are concerned about Joseph Smith's dead Mormons, let me assure you that *he* did not care about any of them. Not his brother. Not his wives. Not his pixie slaves. It's too bad your husband brought him back to life."

Mili didn't dispute Osmodeus's cruel words about Joseph Smith. But her adrenaline shot up realizing that the demon knew who slaughtered the Mormons *and was truly not going to tell her*. Could she get the tiniest clue out of him?

"Do you know for a fact who the evil people were who massacred the inhabitants of Smith Town?" she asked.

Osmodeus answered slowly, enunciating his words quietly and clearly.

"They were not evil. In fact, they did what they did because they thought polygamy—with slave girls—was reprehensible. They cleansed Smith Town."

"They killed the pixies," Mili protested. "Every last one."

"They were blighted. Stained. Spoiled by Mormon lust."

"Would you have resold them if they hadn't been murdered?"

"I sell pixies everywhere, lady. Lots of men like little girls."

"Even pretend ones?"

"Yes."

Osmodeus waited to see if Mili had any last questions. She did.

"Did you ever meet your father, David, the son of Jesse?"

Osmodeus looked immediately uncomfortable, but answered her question, nonetheless.

"Once." Osmodeus gazed at her, then looked at Moshe. He shook his head and replied to Mili. "And you think *I'm* a slime bag."

He raised his hand and turned his thumb down.

"One more thing," he said ominously. "Everyone in Hell knows that Joseph Smith is back and is trying to buy more pixies. Certain parties with long memories may well pay him a visit before he can complete this deal."

"Are you insinuating that he and his brother are about to be attacked again?" Mili asked.

"Make of my words what you will," Osmodeus responded.

The demon nodded at his driver who got out of the car and opened both passenger doors. Moshe and Mili got out of the Mercedes-Maybach without a word. The driver put the car through a long U-turn and drove back down the road out of the kibbutz.

"What a beast," Mili commented. "But I'm glad that we didn't have to shoot him. I want to find Joseph Smith and shoot *him*."

"Sounds like someone else intends to save you the trouble," Moshe said. "Do you suppose Osmodeus himself is arranging a new raid because he hates Smith, too?"

"No," Mili answered. "He's just shrewd. If Smith is killed before he receives the pixies, Osmodeus keeps the little angels *and* the money."

"Where did Joseph Smith get three million dollars?" Moshe asked.

"Never heard of tithing?" Mili answered.

"Are you serious?" Moshe responded truly stunned.

"There were already a hundred thousand tithing Latter-Day Saints in Utah only a few years after Joseph's death," Mili told him. "Every Mormon gives ten percent of their money directly to the church every year. Money easily funneled down to Hell by demons."

"So," Moshe concluded, "Joseph Smith is buying guns and gals. The vigilantes who canceled his enterprise the first time may already be preparing for the next massacre. And we don't have the vaguest idea who they are."

Mili looked at her watch. It was almost two o'clock. She needed to join Mardie and head back to her twin's house in New Babylon. Pfotenhauer would take Little Mardie to the kibbutz and when he returned, he'd drive her and Mardie to eat barbequed steaks and drink whiskey with Wyatt Earp and his brothers.

For tonight she'd put the Mormon investigation on the back burner. And put dining out with three handsome men on the front burner. She had no doubt that Mardie—hungover or not—would approve of her plan.

CHAPTER SEVENTEEN

Pfotenhauer was driving Mili and Mardie along country roads to the Earp Ranch. It was late afternoon and the mountains were gorgeous. High chaparral bathed in the golden light of the sunset.

"Wow," Mardie commented. "This is as beautiful as anywhere in Hell."

"Are you sure we're supposed to be way out here, Pfot?" Mili asked.

"Yes, ma'am," he answered.

"What directions are you using?"

"The ones on Hell Quest. Bunch of young Google guys killed in a plane crash have been busy mapping and photographing everything down here."

"Why are they down here?" Mardie asked.

"Stealing customer stats and selling them to the Red Mafiya."

"The Russian mob?" Mardie yelped. "How does that work? Some blocky Bolshevik takes his mistress out to dinner in Manhattan, and when the waiter looks at his credit card and asks if he's really Bill Clinton the Mafiya guy flashes a fake New York driver's license and says, 'Yes, I'm Bill Clinton.'"

The Hell Quest route took the Volvo through a high-altitude notch in the mountains and then descended into a beautiful valley.

Barbed wire fences subdivided it into grazing pastures for longhorn beef. Thousands of cattle were spread out across the grasslands. Pfotenhauer approached a large sign at the side of the road with an old-fashioned Indian arrow pointing right that had the words EARP RANCH printed on it.

Pfot turned right onto a narrow-paved road, and after a mile the Earp farmhouse was visible. It was a small house painted yellow with white trim. It had a single-pitched eyebrow-style dormer roof, with three picture windows in the front of the house, a door, and a large porch. Three wooden rocking chairs sat on the porch. They were filled with three tall men wearing black suits.

Pfot pulled up to the house. All three men stood. Wyatt Earp walked down the front steps. He nodded to Pfot who got out of the car and opened the passenger doors. Mili stepped out. She had on a navy-blue wool-blend skirt, a plain white silk blouse, and white flats. Mardie stepped out, wearing a black evening dress that covered her shoulders, but was open in the back. She wore three-inch black heels.

"Mrs. Morningstar," Wyatt greeted Mili with a gentle tone in his voice. "You are so kind to travel all this way." Mili smiled and extended her hand. Wyatt shook it. They shared a firm and friendly handshake. Wyatt turned to Mardie and offered his hand. She shook it vigorously. So much so that Wyatt grinned in surprise. "That's quite a grip you have, Miss Wickett."

"Yes," Mardie acknowledged and smiled. "I grew up with Cockney boys and a good grip warned them not to be putting their hands any place they didn't belong or I'd be breaking their fingers."

Wyatt grinned, entertained both by Mardie's own broad London accident and her teasing words.

"I consider myself warned," Wyatt said.

"Sign of an intelligent gentleman," Mardie replied.

Wyatt led the ladies to the porch and introduced them to the two men standing and waiting. He nodded at the first man, a nice looking, middle-aged man who looked like Wyatt with a squarer face. Clearly kin. His graying hair was neatly parted. His black handlebar moustache was even larger than Wyatt's.

"Mrs. Morningstar, this is my brother Virgil," Wyatt said. Virgil smiled. "Spent most of his life as a lawman, but pneumonia got him in the end." Virgil nodded at both ladies. Wyatt lifted his hand and pointed at the second man, a young and handsome clone of Wyatt himself, with slicked-back dark hair and a cold, black, handlebar moustache. "And this is Morgan, my youngest brother. Though he was ambushed and shot down in cold blood, he managed to relieve the Earth of several shifty-eyed bastards before he passed." Morgan grinned shyly and nodded at the ladies.

Mili introduced Mardie to Wyatt's brothers, and then Pfotenhauer who was standing behind her and Mardie. Wyatt asked him to join them but Pfot demurred, saying the evening belonged to the Earp brothers and the Wickett sisters.

"All right, Mr. Pfotenhauer," Wyatt replied. "But no one misses out on an Earp steak. One will be delivered to you wherever you wait. How do you take it?"

"Medium rare."

Wyatt grinned.

"I mean with whiskey? Or something else?"

"Whiskey. Neat," Pfot replied. "Thank you. But only two fingers. I have precious cargo to protect on the way home."

Wyatt nodded, understanding. Pfot headed back to the car.

Earp opened the door to the ranch house and invited the ladies inside. There was a long hall leading to the back of the house. A parson's table with a lamp stood against one wall. Mirrored sliding doors on the opposite wall hid closet space. The end of the hall opened into a big parlor.

Two large fabric-covered sofas faced each other across a large brown-and-black Oriental carpet. The sofas were done in sunflower prints making a pleasant contrast with the Earth colors of the rug. A large oak coffee table sat between the sofas. There were several over-stuffed brown leather chairs, and occasional tables were located by the sofas and chairs.

Adjacent to the parlor was the dining room. It had a fieldstone fireplace with a white mantel and a large-framed mirror above it. There was a dark-stained oak floor with large beige carpet beneath a long table with a black iron base and a white marble top. A large black iron kerosene-fired chandelier hung from a thick chain above the table.

All in all, the interior was pleasing, simple, and very male. Mili doubted that any of the three men had been reunited down here with their pious and God-fearing wives. Mardie thought a woman's touch would have been helpful. Perhaps a linen tablecloth. Waxed and polished floors. Maybe some vases of flowers. Or some art on the walls.

Wyatt invited the ladies to sit and Mardie and Mili sat together on one of the sofas.

Wyatt sat on the sofa across from them. Virgil and Morgan went into the kitchen and returned with cordials for everyone. Virgil carried a tray with small Czech glasses painted with white-and-gold enamel. Morgan had a cut-glass pitcher and filled the glasses on Virgil's tray. Virgil handed them to the Wickett sisters, gave one to Wyatt, and placed the last two on end tables next to the chairs where he and Morgan would be sitting.

They finished and sat down. Wyatt held out his glass to propose a toast. Everyone lifted their glasses.

"May God bless us, each and every one," he said with emotion in his voice.

Everyone drank.

The drink was cool to the tongue. Then hot to the throat. Mardie turned red and Mili coughed.

"Ouzo," Wyatt announced. "From Greece."

Mardie nodded and Mili kept coughing. Virgil refilled everyone's glasses and brought a glass of water for Mili. She accepted it gratefully.

"Ladies," Wyatt continued. "It is an honor to have you in our home. Virgil, Morgan, myself, and three more of our brothers grew up in a house identical to this one. It was small, humble, and comforting. My mother worshipped us, and my father—who took on a variety of peacekeeping roles in his life—taught us the value of the law and its necessity in regulating society. He instilled in us a belief that the men who upheld it in America's Wild West would be appreciated and remembered forever.

"May I also say that he established in each of us a loyalty to family and a reverence for the Almighty that bound us together in life and continues to bind us in the afterlife." Wyatt lifted his glass high and everyone drank. Mili fared better with her second try, though it was a mystery to her why any sane Greek—let alone bachelor cowboys in the middle of Hell—would drink it. Virgil offered refills again, but only the men nodded yes.

Wyatt continued to share stories about growing up with his brothers. Mili and Mardie learned that after he left home he had lived in various places in the southwest before deciding that he wanted to live, marry, and work in Tombstone, Arizona. He enjoyed telling his tales and often asked Virgil and Morgan to add details about the family and their own lives.

Virgil offered whiskey after the ouzo and Mardie obliged him. Mili passed and was offered a Coca Cola on ice. She accepted. She was sure that it was an Earp family nod towards the weaker sex. Hell with that noise. She enjoyed every sip. Several whiskeys into the visit Morgan asked Mili and Mardie how they liked their steaks prepared. He said that he recommended rare or medium rare, but promised that he would grill them any way they desired. Both twins opted for medium rare and Morgan smiled happily.

Dinner was served on the big marble dining table. Wyatt sat at one end, with Mili on his right and Mardie on his left. Morgan and Virgil sat next to the sisters leaving the other end of the table open.

Wyatt nodded at the empty place and told the women that he and his brothers were saving it for the day their father Nicholas would come and visit.

Mili was touched by that gesture. Her Jewish friends back on Earth had always saved a Passover seat at the table for Elijah, God's prophet and champion. Why not one at this table for a heroic and inspirational father? She remembered that when her friends opened the door and invited Elijah to enter, they also prayed to God to pour out his wrath upon their oppressors and persecutors. She could easily imagine Nicholas Earp leading those kinds of prayers with his boys.

Mardie stared at her plate. A large porterhouse steak covered all of it. On a separate plate was corn on the cob, roasted red potatoes, fresh wheat rolls, and butter. Virgil and Morgan served everyone. Wyatt just drank and talked. His brothers did all the work and seemed to do so with dignity and humility. She figured that they took after their mother and that Wyatt took after his father, though, in fact, he had helped all of them become lawmen just like himself. It was good to be sheriff.

Wyatt offered a prayer thanking God for the bounteous fare and then invited everyone to "dig in." Everyone did. Mili wondered why the Earps continued to show respect and honor to God when it was pretty obvious that they were in Hell for the duration. Whether it was for sins of their youth, or questionable practices as fast-shooting peace officers, she did not know. Point was they did homage to the sovereign of the Universe who most residents of Hell had long ago abandoned. Or had never acknowledged. Mili finally decided to ask about it.

"Mr. Earp," she said, "you appear to be a religious man. May I ask you why that should be the case? I mean, down here?"

Wyatt nodded and answered.

"While I have no regrets about how I lived my life, my inclination to shoot down lawbreakers was not approved by all. And apparently not by the Almighty himself. I did what I thought was right. But the final judgment on my actions was God's decision, not mine."

Wyatt's face was at ease, and he shared his thoughts without a hint that things should be any different than they were.

"I and my brothers were raised to accept God's will no matter how it fell on our deeds. To this day I appreciate that the Lord made me strong and unafraid to carry out justice. Just because he has put me down here does not mean I will turn my back on my obligation to honor his name, but will continue to carry out his precepts the best I can."

Both Virgil and Morgan nodded.

"My father and mother are in Heaven," Wyatt continued. "As are our wives, and three of our brothers. James, the eldest, Warren, and Newton. Some surprises there, but who am I to question Jehovah? Sometimes I think that Virgil, Morgan, and I were placed in Hell to assist the Almighty in eliminating troublemakers who are determined to stretch or break the rules down here."

"Isn't that Lucifer's job?" Mili asked keeping her tone polite.

"I don't rightly know, ma'am," Wyatt answered straightforwardly. "To be honest, things down here remind me a lot of the Old West. Plenty of characters. Plenty of guns. And no real marshals or sheriffs. I'd be happy to stand down if there was clear evidence that Lucifer was actively involved in keeping Hell clean and tidy."

Wyatt cut some pieces off his steak. Everyone ate in silence for a moment. Then Mili restarted the conversation.

"Can you give me an example when you felt that you needed to stand up for law and order here in Hell?" Mili asked.

"Of course," Wyatt answered putting down his knife and fork and folding his hands.

"Many years ago," he began, "more than I can accurately remember to be honest, a town was founded by the Mormon leader Joseph Smith and his brother Hyrum Smith. I didn't know about the place at that time since it was located far from here. In those days unless you hobnobbed with demons there was very little information available about other peoples' business.

"The little I heard about any damned souls down here I heard from my late-night drinking pal, Doc Holliday." Wyatt paused. He ran his finger over his bristle moustache, then looked at Mardie. "I heard, by the way, that you had the pleasure of meeting John not long ago."

"I did indeed," Mardie answered. "He saved my life."

"He'd say it was just his obligation," Wyatt commented. "It's the kind of service we all feel obliged to render when called upon."

Mardie nodded and waited for Wyatt to continue.

"Word came that the leader of the Latter-Day Saints had taken to himself some single ladies from New Babylon. That was fine with me. Many women needed a helping hand. Hell was a harder place back when. I remembered that Muhammad the Prophet had taken it upon himself to marry just those kind of women in order to offer them a home, so I had no objection to Joseph Smith having more than one wife.

"But over the years I got word that Smith had somehow managed to bring *young* women—girls really—into his town, yet required that every man besides himself remain single. Smith 'married' these girls in an effort to procreate and build an empire of heirs. Now I don't know where Lucifer was while Smith was practicing intimacy with these young girls, but I decided that Hell was not going to experience that kind of depravity."

"So, you decided to raid Smith Town and kill all the inhabitants," Mili suddenly accused Earp in a harsh tone.

"Heaven forbid!" Wyatt objected. "Virgil, Morgan, myself, and Doc Holliday made up our minds to lead like-minded men to the Mormon settlement and *free* all of those girls."

Mili was stunned.

"And it all went wrong," Wyatt admitted shaking his head. "It all went terribly wrong."

CHAPTER EIGHTEEN

"Will you tell me what happened?" Mili asked Wyatt Earp.

"Doc brought word that the Mormon settlers had been settled in for a decade and did not expect a confrontation with Hell's inhabitants, though John was also told by a demon gunrunner that the Mormons had taken delivery of several dozen Winchester rifles when they first settled their new town. Doc immediately ordered two dozen Colt .44s from another demon gunrunner and a Colt .36 for himself. It was new, lighter, and easier to hide in a card game."

Wyatt smiled a thin smile.

"Do you know that Doc was a celebrated gambler in the Old West?" he asked.

Mili and Mardie both shook their heads.

Wyatt went on.

"When I first met him in Dodge City, he had just won $40,000 at cards. In modern times that would be about a million dollars. Never saw man do better at cards. Anyway, after the demon delivered the Colts, we armed about twenty men and prepared to ride to the Mormon town.

"Doc approached the Mormons first and informed Joseph Smith that a group of citizens was coming to ask for the release of the girls in the settlement. Smith listened to Holliday politely enough. Then he told him those females were his brides and anyone attempting to steal them would be shot on sight. Smith told that to Doc while he stood facing him holding a Winchester rifle. Several men from the town stood next to him also armed with Winchester rifles."

Wyatt paused for a moment and cut himself a piece of steak. He chewed it, then swallowed the last of his whiskey. Morgan jumped up and filled his glass immediately. He topped off Mardie's, then his and Virgil's. Last he brought a fresh glass of Coca Cola for Mili and an extra bottle of the soda pop. After Virgil sat down, Wyatt went on with his story.

"Doc came back and warned us. I nodded. I had never run from a gunfight in my Earthly life and I was not about to start then. We rode from here and reached Smith Town in the late afternoon two days later. At five hundred yards we were subject to the first rifle fire. We just rode harder and entered the town without losing a single man. We got off our horses and protected ourselves by hiding in doorways, crawling on the ground, and slipping around buildings until we got to the city's town hall.

"Standing in front of the building were Joseph Smith and Hyrum. They held their rifles, but didn't use them. Instead, concealed snipers opened fire on us and our men began going down. We in turn began picking off the shooters, targeting them in windows, doorways, and on roofs where they had taken positions.

"Joseph Smith finally held his arm up and the firing stopped. By my reckoning, half our men were dead, and a lot of the Mormon men had been killed as well. I walked up to the Smith brothers with Morgan on one side and Virgil on the other. At ten paces I stopped and called out Joseph Smith.

"'We've come for the girls,' I told him. 'No need for you to die. Just give us the children.'

"'They are my wives, you ignorant savage,' Smith called back. 'They would rather die than be separated from me.'

"'With God as my witness,' I answered him, 'you are a damned mad man.'

"Smith raised his rifle but Morgan reacted quicker and shot him in the chest. He fell to the ground. Hyrum raised his rifle, but Doc shot him dead.

"Suddenly we heard a fuselage of shots coming from inside the courthouse. We all ran after Virgil who burst the doors open with his shoulder. In front of us lay the corpses of the women and children who had been Joseph Smith's wives. Four men turned their rifles towards us and we shot them to pieces. Doc took a bullet in the arm. Morgan got one in the leg. The rest of us were not wounded. All four of the executioners were shot dead.

"All of the women were dead as well. Shot point-blank in the foreheads or temples. Smith had obviously ordered them to be slaughtered rather than be captured by the enemy. I stood in horror. I had never seen anything so heart-wrenching in my life. We gathered up the bodies—our men, Mormon men, all the women and girls—and buried them all in a common grave. We burned the town down and prayed to God with one fervent accord that we would never see the likes of such people again."

"And now you have," Mili said softly.

Wyatt didn't respond. He just sat and drank his whiskey as Virgil and Morgan cleared the table and then brought coffees and homemade chocolate chip cookies (actually Morganmade) for Mili, Mardie, and Wyatt. They served themselves last, but were surprised that the whole plate of cookies had already been eaten.

Wyatt apparently didn't notice or care, but Mardie had watched Mili hastily consume a dozen cookies. Mardie knew that her sister's almost panicked consumption of the sweets had little to do with sugar. It had everything to do with her anxiety over being the person who had asked Lucifer to restore the long-vanished Hellions of Joseph and

Hyrum Smith. And now to her great dismay she had found out the true story of their earlier demise.

"Thank you for telling me what happened," she told Wyatt. "Painful to hear."

"Painful to tell," Wyatt admitted. "I haven't spoken about it since it all went down.

A true tragedy."

"It wasn't your fault."

"I appreciate you saying that, Mrs. Morningstar. I had no idea the kinds of perverse activities Joseph Smith was capable of. By the time I did and reacted, it wound up costing a lot of innocent females' lives." Wyatt paused and looked at Mili. "I don't know if Smith's new order of guns has arrived. I also don't know when the pixies he ordered will be delivered. Doc Holliday drinks and gambles with a lot of well-heeled demons and *they* seem to know everything. John is in New Babylon even as we speak, gambling, but also trying to find out any news about what the Smiths are up to. When he knows, I'll know. And then Virgil, Morgan, and I will ride."

Mili drank her coffee topped up with sugar and cream and ate all of the cookies on the plate that Virgil had refilled. If Wyatt rode out with his brothers and met up with Doc Holliday, they would only have to face Joseph and Hyrum Smith by themselves. The brothers had no Mormon reinforcements yet. But they would shortly have their new Winchester rifles, so there was a good chance that both Earps and Smiths would die. Maybe this time she'd leave well enough alone and let them all stay dead.

* * *

It was a late-night ride home for Mili and Mardie. Neither Wickett sister was sleepy. Wyatt Earp's stories had unraveled the mystery of

Smith Town's destruction and both women were still shocked by the way the females had been dispatched by the men of the town when they were under attack by Wyatt Earp and his vigilantes.

Pfot drove silently. Mili and Mardie talked.

"I personally think we should let Wyatt shoot the shit out of the Smiths," Mardie said angrily. "Trash swept out the door."

"We're talking about *people* here," Mili reminded her.

"Are we?" Mardie shot back. "If you are a traitor to your country, you lose your life. If you're a traitor to *humanity*, why shouldn't you lose your life then, too?"

"Our task," Mili answered sternly, "was to find out how the settlers in Smith Town were massacred. It is *not* to administer our perceived version of justice."

"Then let's just stay out of it," Mardie said angrily. "The Smiths aren't going to change and neither are the Earps. I would suggest that you lay out what we've discovered to Lucifer, and let *him* decide what he wants to do."

Mili gazed at her sister. Despite the fact that she was royally pissed, that really was the right advice. Satan would likely shut down the trafficking in pixie slaves and put the gun-running demons out of business as well. And what about the Smiths and the Earps? He'd probably just let whatever scenario that was destined to happen between them happen. Was that so bad? Maybe it was if Joseph Smith survived. But without pixies and his weapons confiscated, maybe he'd straighten out somehow.

Right. There were those who made things better in Hell, like David Ben-Gurion and Moshe Dayan. And there were those who made things worse, like Joseph and Hyrum Smith. And where did the Earps fit into that black-and-white scenario? Maybe in the same area that Mili and Mardie occupied. They had shot Jack the Ripper. Mardie had killed Eilers the demon. And their investigations had led to several dishonest bankers and smugglers being taken down and assassinated.

Like the twins, the Earps stood for what was right and let the bodies fall where they may. Wyatt was correct when he compared Hell to the Old West. Only the strong survived. And when there were conflicts, who won out didn't come down to who was good or bad, but who was the best shot.

"You're right," Mili finally told Mardie. "It's time to tell everything to Lucifer and then stand back."

"And make sure that Wyatt and the boys have plenty of bullets when they ride," Mardie added.

Mili leaned over and hugged Mardie. Her sister was truly a roughneck. But her heart was always in the right place.

* * *

Lucifer listened carefully to everything his wife shared about the Smiths and the Earps, past and present. He was having a late coffee at Mardie's house where he, Mili, and the children—except for Little Mardie—were staying. He had listened to what both Wickett sisters had to share, and while he was disturbed about the circumstances of the slayings of the Mormon women and pixies, he had no qualms about the fact that Wyatt Earp was going to ride into Mormon perdition once again.

Mardie refilled the Devil's cup with black coffee and he drank it. He was wearing white slacks, a powder-blue Polo shirt, and red Dockers. Both Mili and Mardie were wearing bath robes and drinking their coffee.

"I have heard of the demon Osmodeus," Lucifer said. "I'll have Samns track him down. Hopefully, they'll intercept him before he drops the dozen pixies to Joseph Smith. I'll also make sure the box of new Colt .44 Pythons I received gets to the Earps before they set out."

He looked at Mili and then at Mardie.

"Will Doc Holliday ride with Wyatt and his brothers again?" he asked.

"Wyatt didn't say it," Mardie spoke up. "But I think he intends to have Holliday join him as well."

Mili nodded.

"Very likely," Satan agreed. "Same exact fellas who took on the Cowboys at the OK Corral. All the bad guys died but one and none of the good guys. Maybe that will be the case again. Have to tell you though, this isn't goddamn Tombstone. Whoever isn't standing at the end of this conflict is done—and I don't care if it's Mormons or Earps lying dead on the ground—I'm not bringing anyone back."

Lucifer headed for bed. So did Mardie. But Mili stayed up and made several phone calls. She called Moshe Dayan first. He updated her on the Smith brothers' activities.

"Joseph and Hyrum have camping gear and are setting up miles beyond the citrus orchards. They requested help from the kibbutz. Ben-Gurion declined and he has folks keeping an eye on them."

"Your people are not armed, are they?"

"No."

"Make sure they are out of the way before any shooting starts."

"Shooting?"

Mili filled Moshe in on the role of the Earps in the original massacre and their vow to be involved again.

"Lucifer is going to allow such a thing?"

"Yes," Mili answered. "Don't put your money on the Smiths."

Doc Holliday called on his smart mobile phone. His image came on the screen when Mili answered.

"*You* have a mobile phone?" Mili asked surprised.

"Why not?" he asked. "Do I look like an Earp?"

"Well," Mili responded, "if it walks like a duck, and shoots like a duck—"

"Very funny," Doc said cutting her off. "I wanted you to know that word here in New Babylon is that the Smiths are now armed with Winchesters. I called Wyatt at the ranch and he, Virgil, and Morgan are riding out today. Wyatt said they'd overnight in New Babylon and head to the new Mormon camp the day after that. I figure that by then the Smiths will be ready and waiting for them."

"Are you joining them?"

"If it walks like a duck, and shoots like a duck—"

"Don't get your duck butt shot off," Mili told him.

"Amen," Holliday said.

Mili called Pfot and asked for a ride to the Ben-Yehuda Kibbutz tomorrow at ten. The last communication she got was a text from Lucifer. He had spoken to Doc Holliday and arranged for the once-upon-a-time dentist to take delivery of the dozen Colt Pythons the Devil had asked for. He told Mili that he himself would not be at the confrontation between the Earps and the Smiths and hoped that she would stay away as well. He didn't ask her not to, however. After more than twenty years of successful marriage with Mili Wickett, he knew better, God love him. And if God didn't, she did.

CHAPTER NINETEEN

Pfotenhauer picked up Mili and Mardie at ten o'clock and arrived at the Ben-Yehuda Kibbutz before ten thirty. Moshe Dayan met them in front of the public buildings. The Wickett sisters were wearing jeans, dark T-shirts, and the heavy boots they wore when they worked on Moshe's dig. Mardie wore a navy New York Yankees baseball cap. Mili wore a white Panama plantation hat with a tan leather strap around the bottom of the crown. Both women carried small backpacks.

Moshe hugged them and offered to take their packs.

"Not mine," Mardie replied.

"Not mine either," Mili said. "But thank you."

Moshe glanced at both backpacks.

"You didn't bring snacks in those did you?"

Moshe did not really expect an answer. He was sure that both sisters had handguns in their knapsacks. It was oddly comforting—ex-military man that he was—to know that even if the Wicketts didn't participate in the Earp brothers' take-down of the Smiths, folks at the kibbutz would have some protection if things went south.

"Nope," Mardie told him. "No snacks." Then she reached into her pack and pulled out her new Colt .44 Python. Moshe's eye grew wide. "We're going to *observe* the Earp brothers' confrontation with the Smith brothers. You, too?"

"Yes," he answered.

"Then take one of my guns," Mardie offered. "I have two vintage Colt .44 revolvers that would work well in an experienced hand."

Moshe arched an eyebrow and laughed.

"What?" Mardie demanded irritably.

"Nothing," Moshe said. "I was just thinking that *you* actually could render an opinion on how experienced my hands are."

"Shut up," Mardie said and then laughed. She pulled out both of the Colt six-shooters from her backpack and handed them to Moshe. He examined them while she pulled out a plastic bag full of bullets and gave those to him as well. Moshe put the bullets in his pants pocket and stuck the .44s in the back of his belt.

"Thank you," he told Mardie. "Your new Colt is just for self-defense I assume?"

"Damn straight," Mili answered for Mardie. "We are all strictly onlookers at this showdown. How far is it from the kibbutz to New Babylon? Pfotenhauer's demon stoolies told him that the Earps camped on the city's outskirts last night."

"It's thirty-two miles," Moshe answered.

"Wyatt, Doc, and two Earp brothers chose to ride horses. So, it's likely they won't be here tomorrow."

"Any word on the delivery that Joseph Smith is expecting?" Mili asked.

"We have excellent information on the whereabouts and activities of the slave trader Osmodeus," Moshe told her.

"How was that sourced?" Mili asked.

"Some of our teens hacked his mobile phone."

Mili smiled with delight.

"So, where is Osmodeus?" she asked.

"He's on his way with ten pixies. He's coming here as he does not know that the Smiths have set up alternative living arrangements."

"Who's going to meet him?" Mardie asked.

"We are," Moshe told her. "Osmodeus never carries weapons so there will be no need for violence."

"Once he discovers that the Smiths aren't here, what then?" Mili asked.

"I have instructed all kibbutz workers—men and women, no children—that they are to converge here when they receive a preset signal on their mobile phones indicating that Osmodeus has arrived. He is driving a Hummer today that he keeps in New Babylon."

"And then?" Mili asked, not visualizing what Moshe was planning.

"When Osmodeus drives up we'll surround his vehicle and take the pixies away from him. He's been paid in advance. So, any issues the Smiths have will be with us."

"Sounds like a foolproof plan," Mardie responded.

"Yes, and those are the ones that always seem to go wrong," was Mili's pessimistic take.

"We'll find out soon enough," Moshe remarked. "Osmodeus has turned onto the road leading here. I have activated the signal for the kibbutzniks to gather immediately."

Moshe pointed down the drive. A black Hummer with the paint fried off the hood was approaching. As it pulled into the large open area in front of the kibbutz, hundreds of residents converged on the lot. There were kitchen workers in white aprons. Orchard hands in jeans and blue long sleeve work shirts. Men and women from the truck gardens in shorts, tank tops, T-shirts, and boots. The kibbutz residents circled the Hummer and waited for Moshe to act.

The Hummer's driver-side door opened and Osmodeus stepped out. He was wearing purple shorts, a pink cotton turtleneck, and white Birkenstocks. He waved jovially to the crowd and waited for Dayan to approach. The demon's clothes were soaked with perspiration and he wiped his face with a handkerchief.

"Damn hot in that car," were his first words. "You'd think the manufacturer could have afforded to install some decent air conditioning."

Moshe did not respond.

Osmodeus looked at him, glanced at the Wickett sisters next to him, and then surveyed the huge crowd surrounding him.

"Okay, General," he finally addressed Moshe. "Is it fair of me to assume that you are proposing that I deliver the pixies to you and not the Smiths?"

"You can say it any way you like," Moshe answered. "We are taking custody of your pixies."

Osmodeus waved his arm and a side car door slid open. A large blue demon stepped out. He stood to one side and a bunch of pixies piled out quiet and fearful. They were pretty and petite, but they were not children. They were small beings with intelligent faces and adult postures wearing colored cotton shifts and white sandals. Some had short hair. Others wore it long over their shoulders.

They stood together without speaking. Their eyes flitted back and forth between Osmodeus and Moshe, then gazed anxiously at the crowd gathered around them. Paula Ben-Gurion led several women towards them. Her intent was to bring the pixies into the kibbutz. Before she could reach the little creatures, a series of gun shots echoed in air. Everyone cowered and scores of people hit the ground.

Joseph and Hyrum Smith walked through the crowd and halted a few feet from Moshe and the Wickett sisters. They were dressed in black suits and had Winchester rifles leveled at the crowd.

Moshe walked directly up to them. Hyrum lifted his rifle and aimed it directly at Moshe's chest. Dayan kept walking until he was within three feet of Hyrum.

"What's going on here, Mr. Dayan?" Joseph asked in a calm and civil tone.

"The pixies are not going with you," Moshe said simply.

"But they're mine," Joseph replied.

"I know you *think* that," Moshe replied as Mili and Mardie walked up and stood on either side of him with their Colts drawn. "But we are liberating them. They are slaves no longer."

"You have no right!" Joseph protested, his face instantly flushed and furious. He looked at Osmodeus. "You have broken the contract, demon."

Osmodeus spread his arms wide as if to say, take a good look around you.

Mili spoke up. She looked directly at Joseph Smith.

"Lucifer, who is the Lord and Master of Hell, has Samn demons coming for Osmodeus right now. He has been operating in Hell illegally. Any contract that you made with him is null and void." She nodded toward the big demon. "Osmodeus knows all this to be true. Why don't you ask him for a refund?"

Joseph Smith stared at Mili knowing full well that she was the wife of Hell's sovereign. There wasn't anything he could do except surrender the pixies and both he and Mili knew it. Hyrum didn't see it that way. He swung his Colt toward Mili and put his finger on the trigger.

Oh Jesus, she thought. Here we go again.

Out of the clear blue, Wyatt Earp rode his horse into the crowd. He was holding a new Colt Python revolver. Dressed in a leather shirt, rawhide chaps, and wearing a white Stetson hat he turned his pistol toward Hyrum Smith and shot him in the chest. Three times. As rapidly as he could pull the trigger. When Hyrum fell, Joseph threw his rifle down and put his hands in the air.

Mili stared at Wyatt. He had obviously used a space bridge—as Albert Einstein called them—to surprise the Smiths. Virgil and Morgan materialized out of the air right behind him. They had Colt Pythons as well and rode forward, followed by Doc Holliday who rode in mounted and armed as well.

Wyatt surveyed the unusual scene. Mili and Mardie were next to Moshe Dayan. Osmodeus the demon slave master stood silent and alone. A group of frightened little pixies were surrounded by a group of protective women. And hundreds of kibbutz folk steadfastly encircled everyone in the center.

Earp looked at Joseph Smith.

"You don't seem to have a lot of options, Mr. Smith," he said without trying to sound demanding or threatening.

"I know who you are Wyatt Earp," Smith answered and lowered his hands. "And I have learned that you were the criminal who led the mob that murdered the men, women, and children of Smith Town. Did you think that God didn't see?"

"No one saw that, Mr. Smith," Wyatt answered. "Because that's not what happened. Your own men slaughtered the women and the pixies in your settlement. We punished those murderers and buried all the sad victims of Smith Town. And for two hundred years we were at peace until you were allowed to return."

"And I'm not leaving again," Smith cried, his voice filled with fury. "I stand before you without sin!"

"Don't think so," Mili said and hit Smith's forehead with the butt of her gun. As he collapsed, Wyatt reached down and swept the unconscious man over the front of his saddle.

"We need a hard-working hand at the ranch," he commented.

Before anyone else could say anything, Earp removed his hat, bowed his head towards Mili and Mardie, then replaced his hat and trotted into the space bridge and was gone. The Earp brothers, Morgan and Virgil, and Doc Holliday disappeared behind him.

Mili looked down at the dead body of Hyrum Smith. She wondered who was better off? Hyrum or his abducted brother?

Seemed to Mili that either way no one would be hearing from the Smith brothers for a long time.

* * *

Moshe led a work detail that buried Hyrum in the old Mormon bone pit. Mili and Mardie participated. After Hyrum was interred the rest of the skeletons from the last raid were reburied and the excavation trenches and pits of the Smith Town dig were covered over. No one said a prayer.

Mili and Mardie showered and met Moshe at his apartment. They sat in Dayan's kitchen drinking coffee and trying to come to grips with what had happened.

"None of this is in any way satisfying," Mili said clearly depressed.

"You solved a very difficult case," Moshe told her. "There's that."

"Right," she answered sarcastically. "I encouraged Lucifer to bring back the Smiths, only to see one of them killed and the other kidnapped."

"Satan supported you then," Mardie told her. "And however he deals with Joseph Smith, the Earps, and Doc Holliday, it's out of your hands."

Mili stared glumly at her sister.

"So, what are you telling me?" she asked.

"It's time to move on," Mardie said bluntly. "Like you have moved on after every other case you've solved down here. Put it behind you. Move on."

Mili's mobile phone rang. She reached in her purse and pulled it out. She saw Lucifer's face on the screen and answered. She stood up and walked outside.

"Hello, Lu," she said. "Bet you've already heard about everything that happened here."

"I have," Lucifer answered. He paused and looked tenderly at his wife. "It's taken a toll on you, hasn't it?"

"It was brutal. Wyatt stopped Hyrum from shooting me, and Moshe and the wonderful people here at the kibbutz stood together and saved the pixies. Have to say though, solving this crime was harder and less satisfying than anything I ever experienced at Scotland Yard. I feel worn out."

Lucifer nodded sympathetically.

"You'll have to weigh your future involvement in any crimes that lie ahead in Hell's future. I can't help you with that. However, I can provide some solace, if you wish. Some medicine for melancholy."

Mili smiled a wan but grateful smile.

"Come home, love," Lucifer told her. "Take a break from being one of the Wickett sisters and come home to me."

Mili nodded, her eyes filling with tears. She finished the call and punched in Pfot's number to arrange a ride back to Mardie's house.

She turned to Moshe.

"I'm going home," she announced, then hugged him hard.

She looked at Mardie.

"Coming?"

"Yes," Mardie answered. She smooched Moshe's cheek and turned to Mili. "What in the world will we do now that *this* whole thing is over?"

Mili looked at Mardie and thought about that.

"I've been enjoying going to reenactments with you again," she said.

"Ditto," Mardie said enthusiastically. "This coming week the club is restaging *Moses in the Court of Pharaoh*."

"The very first play we ever saw?"

"Yes!" Mardie exclaimed. "The one with the snakes! There's a new Moses though. New snake, too. The last one swallowed the original Moses and the actor quit once they cut him out."

Mili grinned.

"Of course," Mardie went on, "we could also go bowling—"

Mili instantly interrupted her sister.

"Call Bowles and ask him to get us tickets to the Moses revival," she said. "Do any of this season's reenactments feature guns?"

"No!" Mardie said. "What are you thinking? All the performances are based on Bible stories."

"In that case let's get seats to all of them."

Mili truly longed for a whole season—in the club and in Hell as well—where there would be no guns, no bullets, no shootings, no murders, no cases, no investigations, and no deaths. If she'd been writing memoirs about her adventures down here, this next installment would be entitled *The Wickett Sisters on Vacation.* Wouldn't be very exciting though, she realized.

Woo hoo!

The End

Acknowledgements

I would like to thank the many wonderful readers who have made the Wickett Sisters part of their lives, and especially my great friends who read early drafts of this manuscript and gave valuable advice as well as happy approval of the cover art: Margie Cleland, Mardell Haggard, Trace Jones, Sheridan Oakes, and Elizabeth Wagner.

And to acknowledge the dedicated professionals who make books out of Mili and Mardie's stories. Ibrahim Zobi for first copy edits; Mark Meyer of Professional Book Proofreading for final copy edits; the formatting artists at Wordzworth; and Vincent Chong for his cover design and art.

Brilliant partners all! Thank you.

www.ingramcontent.com/pod-product-compliance
Lightning Source LLC
Chambersburg PA
CBHW071529120726
47907CB00013B/1272

9781639448869